CAFFEINE N

C000264203

Suits and Bullets

ALFIE ROBINS

Fiction aimed at the heart
and the head...

Published by Caffeine Nights Publishing 2016

Published in Great Britain by
Caffeine Nights Publishing
4 Eton Close
Walderslade
Chatham
Kent
ME5 9AT

www.caffeinenights.com

British Library Cataloguing in Publication Data.

A CIP catalogue record for this book is available from the British Library

ISBN: 978-1-910720-59-2

Cover design by

Mark (Wills) Williams

Everything else by
Default, Luck and Accident

For Sue

Chapter 1

For Detective Constable Greg Warren, it had been one of those days. To be fair he'd had a total pig of a year. How did that television news presenter put it, 'a long way from home, wet through and pissed off'? Well that was Greg Warren; he was well and truly pissed off. The satnav of life was leading him absolutely nowhere but around in ever decreasing circles. He was virtually disappearing up his own arse.

Warren was a solitary kind of a bloke, not that he found it hard to make friends, he just preferred his own company. During the course of his career he had proved to be a hard man who didn't suffer fools gladly, a man good with his fists and feet in a tough situation.

Perhaps that was part of the reason there was no one at home to have a hot meal and a glass of wine waiting, when he returned after a hard day. To be totally honest his life was the pits. That's why he decided a move up north might do him some good.

The Detective Constable took the initiative and moved to the 'grim' north, leaving behind his parents and a few mates. They told him 'work hard, keep your head down and you'll crack it', promotion that is, three months – six months max, wrong, totally wrong. He was floundering and almost a year on he was contemplating moving back down to the 'smoke'. He looked up from his computer screen, his boring colleagues looked to be busy, with the exception of Baz, the office loon who was trying to impress the new temp, her arse hanging over her chair like a small country. She looked more interested in the packet of crisps she was munching her way through.

Warren, was bored out of his brain, his fingers were still on the keyboard, he just stared out of the second floor office window. For some bizarre reason he was taking some enjoyment in watching people dash about in the rain, trying to avoid getting soaked by the passing traffic. That was also the day Detective Constable Greg Warrens' life changed – forever.

Chapter 2

Greg Warren had been working out of a busy nick in central London, pretty close to King's Cross Station. He'd been there since he graduated from Hendon Police College. His probationary period went without hitch, and after three years on the beat he achieved his goal and entered CID. Things went well at King's Cross, he was encouraged by colleagues and passed the Sergeant's Promotion Board, but unfortunately promotion wasn't forthcoming due to the fierce competition in the Metropolitan Police. And that is how he ended up chasing his dream in the arse end of nowhere.

He woke as usual to the shrilling of the alarm clock, 6.30am, the start of another day in the boring life of Greg Warren. Reluctantly, he kicked off the duvet and swung his legs over the side of the bed. With his head in his hands he sat for a moment or two before getting a grip of himself and heading for the bathroom. He took the plunge, stood up and padded barefoot across the cold hardwood flooring. Hands resting on the washbasin, he stared in the mirror studying his face, while the basin filled with hot water. 'Jesus, man you're a fucking mess,' he said out loud to the reflection. There seemed to be more wrinkles than yesterday, even the bags beneath his watery blue eyes looked darker and he was sure his short cropped hair had a few grey streaks mingling with the black. He turned off the tap and immersed his face in the hot water. With water dripping down his face he again checked out the image, maybe a miracle would have improved his lived-in look. It hadn't; the face of a weary man stared back.

There was no doubt about it, he wasn't feeling on top of his game, he thought maybe he was coming down with something. He went back through to the bedroom, dressed, and opened the curtains only to see it was pouring down with rain. Downstairs in the kitchen he switched on the television like he did every morning, and like every other morning he had his predictable breakfast of scrambled eggs on toast washed down with a pot of freshly brewed coffee. Breakfast finished, he stuffed the dirty crockery into the dishwasher, the same as he did every other morning. Sitting on a kitchen chair, he put on his shoes and gave them a quick buff with a duster – he liked shiny shoes. He walked across to the built-in oven, checked his reflection in the glass door and straightened his tie, then picked up the remote and killed the television. 'Up and at 'em,' he said out loud and left for work.

Most days, Warren made the journey into work by bus, but due to the crappy weather he decided to take the car. 'C'mon, get moving,' he shouted out loud as he sat in congested traffic. No one heard. He wished he'd caught the bus after all. By the time he reached Hull's Central Police Station in the town centre his stress levels had moved up a level. He felt as if he'd done a day's work even before he signed in. Warren parked up in the designated Police parking spaces in the nearby multi-storey car park, locked the car, pulled up the collar of his jacket, and taking the concrete stairs to the ground floor two at a time he made a beeline for the station.

He punched the security code into the back door lock, nodded to the uniformed officers on the custody desk and made his way up a floor to the CID room.

'Morning Greg, how's it going?' asked one of his colleagues.

'Not bad mate, I'm fed up with the weather though. Came in the car and it was bumper to bumper all the way here.'

'What are you on with?'

'Still playing catch up with my paperwork from last week, trying to get it done before the DI gives me a rollicking.' His colleague rolled his eyes knew the feeling well.

Two hours later, with a congealing mug of cold coffee in front of him his mood still hadn't improved. He was still sat at his computer typing up incident reports and other mundane crap that he'd let mount up over the past few days when a voice whispered in his ear. 'The Super wants a word – now.' It was Detective Inspector Bill Grimes.

'What have I done this time, boss?' he asked pushing back in his wheeled chair. 'Another bollocking?'

'No idea Greg, just passing on the message – don't keep him waiting,' he patted Warren on the shoulder and disappeared back through his office door, not giving him a second glance.

He couldn't recall doing anything worth being summoned into the inner sanctum for, not recently anyway. He freed his jacket from the back of his chair and put it on, and for the second time that morning he straightened his tie. Two flights of stairs up, he stood before the boss's secretary like a schoolboy waiting to be told off for smoking. Frosty Face, the Super's gate keeper looked up from her work, even though Warren gave her his best smile she didn't say a word. Remaining pan-faced she picked up the phone and held a short whispered conversation. 'You can go in now,' she said giving him the evil eye that would have turned a lesser man to stone, and returned to tapping away at her computer keyboard.

He knocked on the door and entered the office. The smell of furniture polish invaded his nostrils, not the cheap spray stuff but the expensive smell of bee's wax and lavender. Superintendent James Pratt sat behind his highly waxed mahogany desk; he wasn't alone in the office. Two suspicious looking suits were keeping him company. The suits didn't even acknowledge that Warren had entered the office. The Super inclined his head to a vacant chair. Warren sat down, folded his arms across his chest, and crossed his legs out in front of him. No recognition from the suits, *well,* he thought, *if it's a roasting I may as well be comfortable.*

'Right gentlemen, I'll leave you too it. If you need anything just ask Suzie on the desk, she'll sort you out,' the Super picked up his briefcase, put his dress cap under his arm and walked out.

What the hell was going on?

Suit number One stood up and walked around the desk and sat in the boss's chair. Suit number Two stayed where he was. Number One was making a real show of reading the folder that lay open in front of him, like he himself would do in the interview room when he wanted to intimidate a suspect. Warren continued to sit, taking it all in, keeping his mouth shut while he studied his inquisitors. Suit number One was going bald on top and wearing thick-rimmed spectacles, he looked a bit like Ronnie Barker from the 'Two Ronnies', only thinner. Number Two had that worried look of a married man, a man with the world on his shoulders.

Suit number One took out an eight-by-ten-inch photograph from a folder and studied the image, he looked at Warren and then passed the photograph to his colleague. He sat wondering what the hell it was all about. Suit number Two then placed the photograph face down on the desk. He looked at his colleague and nodded, that was when Warren felt the need to say something.

'What the fuck's going on here?'

'Calm down DC Warren, no need for bad language.' Suit number Two then slid the upturned photograph in front of him.

Warren turned it over and picked it up.

'This is bloody mental – why have you been taking surveillance photographs of me? Am I under investigation or something?'

He had a feeling he wasn't going to like the answer.

'Take a closer look DC Warren.'

He did, but he couldn't place where the picture had been taken.

'So, are you going to tell me what's going on?'

He pushed the photograph back across the desk and sat back folding his arms defiantly across his chest.

'The photograph, can you confirm it's you in the picture?'

'Of course I can, who else is it – Mickey Fucking Mouse?'

'What would you say if I said it isn't you in the picture?'

'I'd say you've lost your marbles.'

'DC Warren, the man in the photograph is named Raymond Cole.'

Warren leaned forward and grabbed the picture of the desk and had another look. *Bloody hell*. He couldn't tell the difference. He may not have dressed the way Warren did but the man in the photograph could have been his identical twin. Puzzled, he looked from one suit to the other and back to the photograph, hoping for an answer. None was forthcoming.

'And who *is* Raymond Cole when he's at home, and where is all of this leading to?'

'All in good time.'

'DC Warren, we have a proposition for you…' Suit number Two this time.

'Stop right there, what's going on here and who the hell are you? National Crime Force? MI5? Spooks?'

Warren was trying unsuccessfully to keep command of the situation. He was losing.

'None – and all of the above?' Suit number One said non-committal.

'Not much of an answer…'

'DC Warren, please shut up and listen.' Warren did as he was told and sat back in his chair once more. 'As I was about to say, we have a proposition for you. When we've finished explaining you can ask all the questions you want – if we *answer* your questions is a different matter. First, stick your head out that door and ask the young lady outside – Suzie – very nicely to bring in some coffee.' Warren thought calling Frosty Face a young lady was pushing it a bit; he kept the thought to himself and did actually go and ask for the coffee.

'So what's this all about?' He asked as he took up his seat once again.

'As we've said, all in good time,' suit number Two replied.

Suzie duly arrived with a loaded tray of coffee and biscuits. The crockery rattled, as she unceremoniously put the tray down on the desk, ignored Warren, smiled at the suits and left without a word. Suit number Two poured out three cups.

'Help yourself to milk and sugar.'

Warren sat forward in his chair, put a splash of milk and two sugars in his coffee and sat back, holding his cup and saucer balanced on his knee.

'Ok, I'm listening,' he said as he settled back, nursing his coffee.

If Warren was honest he was intrigued to hear what they were going to say.

'Raymond Cole, born 5th June 1987 in Leeds, an only child and both parents died when he was four years old, consequently he was brought up by his grandparents – both deceased.'

Suit number Two took his turn. 'He's a player in the arena of arms smuggling, drug importation and he's also been known to have accepted the odd contract hit or two. But he does have some scruples and draws the line at the trafficking of young women.'

'Sounds like a nice bloke,' Warren said with an edge.

'Most of the time he's on the periphery, he's not exactly big time, but he does have his moments. More importantly, he does have access to bigger fish. All in all, a small but very important cog in a big wheel.'

'Where do I come into it?'

By now Warren was more than little intrigued.

'Remember last month, when you travelled by North Sea Ferries on that stag weekend mini-break to Rotterdam?' Warren nodded. 'You wouldn't believe the panic you caused when you passed through Dutch Customs. Their facial recognition software on their security system flagged you up all over Europe as Raymond Cole.'

'How come I wasn't picked up?'

Warren inwardly smiled at the prospect of being 'a wanted criminal'.

'Simple, your passport scanned correctly and a few clicks on a keyboard and the panic was averted.'

'That's when one of our employees had an idea,' Suit number One said, 'our unit, Europol, and other International Law Enforcement agencies have been looking for a way into the organisation for quite some time, some bright spark thought why not make a substitution?'

'And you thought of me.' *Why did I ever go on that weekend?*

Warren didn't know whether to be flattered or feel that he was being taken for a mug.

'Correct, we thought of you.'

Suit number One sat back in the Super's chair and folded his arms. Suit number Two sat forward resting on his elbows, then turned his head and looked at Warren.

'What we propose is that you take his place.'

There was a prolonged silence. Warren nearly gagged on his coffee.

'Just like that?' he said to break the silence.

'Yes, DC Warren, just like that.'

'So I look like him,' said Warren, 'it doesn't mean I can be him.'

'Oh, but it does.' Suit number One kept his voice low and calm. 'With the right coaching and guidance, we can teach you everything there is to know about Cole, his ways, his friends and his contacts.'

'Do I have any say in this?'

Warren doubted it, he knew a refusal could end any hopes of furthering his career, on the other hand if he accepted, who knew where it could lead?

'The decision is yours entirely. If you say no, we walk away, you won't see us again.'

'Do I have time to think about it?'

'Of course,' Suit number Two pulled back the sleeve of his jacket and looked at his watch. 'Two minutes and counting.'

'If I say yes, what happens next?'

Warren was beginning to warm to the idea.

'We walk out of here together, you on Sergeant's pay scale with immediate effect and preparation will commence.'

'What about my position here?'

'Terminated immediately.'

'And the Super, he's ok with this?'

'All approved from a higher authority than Superintendent Pratt.' Warren sat quietly. Suit number one studied his watch. 'One minute thirty seconds.'

'And I could pull out at any time?'

'We would require your long-term commitment DC Warren, you would be in it for the long haul, from start to completion.'

He checked his watch again. 'Thirty seconds then we're leaving.'

'Ok, I'm game.' *Shit what have I just said?*

'Good to have you on board Detective Sergeant Warren.'

Both suits stood and shook hands with the newly promoted officer. 'Fancy a pint?'

The Georgian pub around the block from Hull's Central Police Station was always busy no matter what the time of day. The place was packed with a mixed clientele, the high flyers having their late business lunches, the leave-work-early crowd having one for the road before heading off home to their families, and the usual out of work hardened drinkers who had been in there since opening time.

Warren and *Suit* number One headed for a booth at the far end of the lounge bar. Number Two went to the bar to order drinks. A few minutes of stilted small talk followed until number Two came across with a tray of drinks, and set them on the table.

'How does this work with Cole?' Warren asked, as he picked up his pint of lager off the beaten copper topped table.

'Mr Cole was discreetly lifted four nights ago in Birmingham, along with two of his closest colleagues as they left an Indian restaurant.'

'Where are they now?'

'Out of sight and out of mind. Cole is enjoying the hospitality of HMP Belmarsh, while his colleagues are enjoying some good old Scottish hospitality – courtesy of HMP Peterhead.'

'Have they been charged?'

'Not yet – maybe sometime – maybe never.'

'And you can do this?'

'Sergeant, we can do what we like.'

He was impressed.

Warren sat quiet, his head full of questions waiting to be asked. 'What happens now?'

'You have your warrant card?' Suit number One asked, holding out his hand. Warren removed his warrant card from his jacket pocket and passed it across.

'Thank you.'

Warren kept his arm extended, holding out his hand. 'A new one?'

'You won't be needing one for a while Sergeant.' This wasn't what Warren expected. He shook his head from side to side, wondering what the hell he'd signed up for. 'And that was the *last* time anyone will call you Sergeant.'

'For the immediate future anyway,' number Two added

'What happens next?'

Suit number Two took a business card out of his jacket pocket and handed it across. 'Be at this address at nine o'clock in the morning.'

The address was a business park in the west of the city.

'By the way,' said Warren, 'what should I call you, sir, guv or what?'

'I'm Bob,' said suit number one 'and he's John.'

'That's it, Bob and John?'

'That's all there is.' They stood up to leave, their drinks hardly touched. 'See you in the morning Greg, or perhaps I should say Mr Cole.'

The three men shook hands and they left. Warren was left nursing his pint wondering what the future was to bring.

'Well that went better than I expected,' Bob said as they made their way back to their vehicle.

'You think he's up to the job?' John asked as he clicked the key fob.

'He's got a good record, a good thief taker.'

Bob climbed in to the front passenger seat of the BMW and strapped himself in.

'Yes, but that's not what I asked,' John said as he settled into the driver's seat.

Bob shrugged his shoulders. 'Granted he's lacking in undercover experience, but as things stand he's the best chance we have. Everyone has to start somewhere, as long as he keeps that temper of his in check I can't foresee any problems.'

'We'll see.' John slipped the car into drive and drove the brand new BMW X6 M out of the station car park.

Philip Martin and Gordon Harrison, AKA John and Bob, had for the past six years headed up a covert intelligence department answerable only to the Home Secretary, it was a department with no name, consequently very few people outside of the Home Secretary's Office knew their real names.

Since its conception the department had enlisted a team of highly experienced skilled individuals from all branches of the uniformed services, drawn from the SAS, SBS, the Parachute Regiment and the Police Force.

Operatives served all over the globe, often alongside their counterparts in other international law enforcement agencies, on occasions necessitating the need to venture deep undercover for prolonged periods in the fight to thwart terrorist organisations or to infiltrate global and home grown organised crime. On the whole, the majority of those enlisted served their time with the department on home ground, working within the borders of the United Kingdom or Europe.

Fighting crime in such shadowy circumstances, with a team of individuals, many of whom were of dubious character, had proved to be very lucrative all-round to those involved. Those who didn't care where the cash came from and knew how to keep their mouths closed were well rewarded. Consequently, John and Bob were now very wealthy men – and they hadn't finished.

Chapter 3

Warren never went back to the office, he collected his vehicle from the multi-storey and picked up a takeaway then spent a lone evening occupied with a multitude of thoughts, a *doppelgänger... undercover... promotion, how the hell had all this happened out of the blue?* Confused, but feeling pleased with the prospect of the 'exciting' opportunities ahead, Warren spent the rest of the evening listening to music – with a bottle of single malt for company, he was too wired for sleep and it was well past midnight before he settled down.

He was already awake when the alarm clock duly rang out at 7.30am. In anticipation of a big day he had taken it easy with the malt, and was in a much better frame of mind than he usually was first thing in the morning. He swung his legs to the floor, sat for a moment and then padded off to the bathroom. He let the beads of the power shower work their magic, towelled himself dry, shaved and went back to the bedroom. He took his best suit from the wardrobe and dressed, white shirt and navy blue tie. Dressed and breakfasted with the obligatory coffee he sat at the kitchen table, glancing at the wall clock every couple of minutes.

'In for a penny in for a pound,' he said out loud to the empty house. Dressed to kill, with his car keys in hand he left the house.

The start of the first day of the rest of his life.

He was puzzled when he arrived at his destination, a non-descript modern, two-storey office unit on the Priory Business Park on the western edge of the city. He knew the area well but was puzzled. 'Can't be right?' he said out loud as he picked up the business card off the passenger seat and checked the address, no mistake. He threw the card back onto the seat. It was the right place. He drove through the security gates into the gravel car park and parked next to two expensive four-wheel drives. He climbed out, locked his car and crunched his way over the gravel. The brass nameplate, fixed on the wall adjacent to the entrance door stated the building was the head office of Gemmell Strategies.

Who the hell are Gemmell Strategies? He was sure it wouldn't be long before he found out. Reaching out with his right hand, he was just about to press the intercom button.

'Just push the door,' a voice said through the speaker grill. 'Straight up the stairs, first door on the right.'

Warren thought he recognised the voice as belonging to Bob. The foyer of Gemmell Strategies was stark, all very institutionalised with no reception desk; no furniture at all, the ambience was made complete with plain magnolia painted walls minus the obligatory Monet prints. As instructed, he climbed the stairs two at a time, his shoes echoing in the empty stairwell. Two doors at the top of the stairs, Warren knocked on the one to the right as instructed and walked in.

'Greg, good to see you, on time as well,' John said looking at his watch as Warren entered the austere office, which was also lacking in any frivolities or personal items.

'Pour yourself a coffee and make yourself comfortable.'

'Morning gents,' Warren said as he looked around the office, scanning for the coffee machine.

Two battered metal frame desks, a bank of filing cabinets lined the length of one wall and a large free-standing whiteboard occupied most of the floor space. The whiteboard covered with eight inch by ten-inch photographs of Raymond Cole. Warren helped himself to coffee, pulled over a chair and sat looking around at the stark surrounding of the functional office. 'Nice place,' he remarked, flippantly.

John walked over to the window and turned around facing into the room. 'Serves its purpose. So, Greg, any doubts?'

'I'd be lying if I said I didn't have any reservations about it, but I made my decision and stand by it. I'm not one to back down on my word,' Warren said with trepidation.

'Glad to hear it.'

Bob sat scanning through a manila folder.

'Your service record, impressive,' he said, closing the folder giving it a pat with the flat of his hand. 'It does seem you let your temper get the better of you on occasions.'

'That's all in the past,' Warren answered.

'Also I noticed you've never had any firearms training? He looked to John, 'nothing that can't be put right?' John nodded his acknowledgement. *Firearms*, Warren raised his eyebrows. It didn't go unnoticed. 'I can't see the situation arising when you may have to use one, but still the training can only stand you in good stead, don't you agree?'

John stood up and walked over to the whiteboard and pointed an outstretched arm at various photographs of who could only be described as Warren's twin.

'Raymond Cole, currently detained in segregation at HMP Belmarsh.' Warren stood up, walked across and joined John by the whiteboard. 'As far as his colleagues are concerned, they will be alerted to the fact that Cole escaped from custody on his way to appearing in court. It will be well publicised, the television news channels, the national papers etc.'

'And me?' asked Warren as he returned to his chair and sat down.

'You my dear chap, you start studying,' John picked up a thick file marked confidential and dropped it into Warren's lap.

'Cheers,' he replied with a twisted smile on his face.

'And may I suggest you lose the suit, Cole is not known for being a snazzy dresser, he's more of a jeans and jacket type of a man.'

Since the day Warren had walked away from Hull Central Police Station he had never had any contact from his former colleagues, not even his former DI had made the effort to get in touch. Whether it was due to officialdom Warren didn't know, but it was obvious they had been warned off. He was now well and truly off the radar. Over the following weeks Warren spent every waking hour learning the ways of another man, in all respects he became Raymond Cole. Gone were the sharp suits, replaced with casual gear bought from chain stores. He walked like Cole, he spoke like Cole, and everything about him oozed Cole. To all intents and purpose he was Cole, and he'd been answering to the name with no hesitation for days.

To help keep things under wraps, Warren underwent his firearms training in Rotherham, with South Yorkshire Police rather than at the local Police range. He had always been somewhat apprehensive about using firearms. Using a lethal weapon was something that had never appealed to him. The thought of taking someone's life turned his stomach, ok, he'd had his fair share of physical altercations before and during his career life, but guns? Being the professional he was and as the new job necessitated the possible use of one, he was determined to do his best.

Warren reported to South Yorkshire Police Firing Range and was kitted out with the standard issue firearms unit uniform of black combat type overalls and 'monkey boots'. Feeling self-conscious in the black uniform, he stood listening intently to ex-Special Forces, Firearms Instructor Sergeant David Dosdale. Warren thought Dosdale to be in his early forties, blond hair turning grey and with piercing blue eyes; he didn't look the type of copper you messed with. Dosdale was to be his instructor for the two-day intensive crash course.

'We're lucky, we have the range to ourselves today,' said Dosdale as he led Warren through a maze of corridors to the firing range. The range had soundproof walls and ceiling, a long counter type top was divided off with partitions making individual firing cubicles. Facing down the length of the range, in front of each cubicle was 100 metres of narrow free area, with a target at the far end worked by an electronic pulley system. Dosdale laid the aluminium case he'd been carrying on the counter top, flicked the catches and opened the case, inside was a firearm, two magazines and two boxes of nine millimetre shells. He picked up the weapon and held it carefully as if it were the crown jewels.

'This is the Sig Sauer P226, a 9mm calibre automatic and it takes a 10-round magazine, it's been around since 1976, tried and tested and it's still a favourite with our Special Forces. The frame is a lightweight alloy and the slide is stainless steel.' Dosdale picked up an empty magazine, clicked it into place, slid the mechanism and passed the weapon over to Warren. 'Don't worry it's not loaded. It can be your friend or your worst enemy, respect is the name of the game, respect your weapon and it will be your friend, treat it badly and well...' He shrugged.

Warren held out his hand and accepted the deadly cold metal firearm.

'Heavy, I wasn't expecting it,' he said as he passed it from one hand to the other as if checking the balance.

'Near enough thirty-four ounces when the magazine's full, slightly heavier with the fifteen round mag.' Warren passed back the Sig. 'Right, grab a hold of these,' he said passing Warren a pair of safety glasses and ear protectors.

Under the instruction of Dosdale, Warren was taught the finer points of the Sig 17. Starting with the firearms safety features, how to hold the weapon competently and how to stand correctly when using a weapon and how to load the magazine.

'You'll have seen the "gangsta" lads holding their weapons like this?' He held the gun one handed at arm's length, the weapon on its side. 'Unpredictable, no strength in the wrist, with the kickback the weapon produces the bullet would probably end up where it wasn't intended. Not good if there are civilians in the vicinity.'

Warren nodded.

'Whenever possible use two hands, like this, it's not only safer but you maintain full control of the weapon.' The instructor demonstrated the correct two handed firing position, holding the grip firmly in both hands, with the trigger finger outstretched in front. He passed the weapon back to Warren to get the feel for it. Once Dosdale was sure he had a full grasp of the safety requirements and felt confident that Warren had the 'feel' for the Sig, they progressed to arming the magazine with live ammunition. Then the live firing demonstration began.

Warren settled himself in the partitioned-off firing booth, and put on the safety glasses and ear protectors. The fully-armed Sig lay on the counter top in front of him. Warren looked down the range at the target 50 metres in front of him. He picked up the Sig and assumed the firing position.

'Straight down the range and watch your target, aim for the body, the largest mass. Single shots in your own time,' said Dosdale.

Warren nodded and aimed the Sig down the firing range towards the paper, taking his time he sighted down the weapon, released the safety catch, took a deep breath and slowly squeezed the trigger. 'Bang', it wasn't like the sound of a television gun, it was a real BANG, loud and deafening even through his ear protectors. The kick-back travelled through Warren's arms and body, he took a deep breath and then he gently squeezed the trigger again, continuing steadily until the magazine was emptied.

Warren cleared the weapon and placed it down on the counter top, while Dosdale pressed a button and an electric motor whirled, bringing the target towards them. Of the ten shots fired, seven had found their mark in the centre mass of the target.

'Not bad,' said Dosdale, 'now reload the magazine and do it again.'

This was repeated again and again until all rounds were within the centre circle. Once he had proved his competence on the firing range, things moved up a level to tactical work. Indoors and outdoors, Warren was placed in combat situations. After two days of intensive training Warren felt comfortable, maybe not quite the expert as Dosdale, but he was pretty confident and to his surprise he found he enjoyed the experience and the respite from the office.

Then it was back to the office of Gemmell Strategies and his studies.

While Warren, or Cole as he had become, was yet again sat watching another DVD of his alter ego, John and Bob sat in the main office discussing his progress.

'What do you think of our lad then, Bob?'

'To be honest John, when we started out I did have reservations about him, but, I have to admit they seem to have been totally unfounded.' He stood up from his desk and walked across to the large window, his hands in his pockets he stood as if he was admiring the view across the River Humber, then turned back to face into the room. 'He's ready.'

'My thoughts exactly, ask him to come through will you?'

John went through to the smaller office where Warren paced up and down, practising his swaggering walk.

'Looking good, Greg,' he said, 'have a minute?'

Warren nodded and followed John back to the main office.

'Sit down,' said Bob, John remained standing.

'Sounds ominous,' said Warren.

'Not at all.' Bob opened the buff coloured folder that lay before him on the desk and started flicking through the pages. 'I would say all the preparation has been taken care of.'

'So, what happens next?' asked Warren, apprehensively.

'We move on to the next stage, or should I say the first stage of the operation, proper,' said John as he walked over and perched on the edge of the desk. 'In approximately one hour's time, Cole will be seen leaving HMP Belmarsh to attend a court appearance in central London. There will be enough distractions made by "our" prison officers in the main building, making it pretty hard NOT to know what was happening.'

Bob took over the story.

'Yes, Cole will be driven out of the prison for approximately two miles, under maximum security, but never leave the vehicle I might add, he will then be driven back to the prison, entering through a secure service entrance. None of the prison population will be any the wiser that he had returned. As far as the inmates on the segregation block are concerned, they will be on lock-down and as far as they will be aware he never left the building.

'Close the blinds will you, John?' Once the blinds had been pulled down, Bob proceeded to turn on the flat screen television and then inserted a DVD into the player. 'This is what will be broadcast on national television this evening, starting with the Six O'Clock News. The relevant television news departments will provide dialogue from a prepared statement they will be issued with.'

John reclaimed his position on the desk edge. Warren turned his chair and watched the screen with interest.

The silent footage started almost immediately. A police patrol vehicle could be seen, turned at right angles blocking the road, a non-descript black Ford Transit van, the type used for the discreet transportation of prisoners lay on its side, the back doors lay wide open. Armed police officers could be seen securing the area.

'As far as the public will be concerned they will be told the escape happened quite by chance after a collision with a builder's skip lorry. Whilst on the other hand, it will be leaked to the criminal fraternity it was a hit. The hit organised and pre-planned and Raymond Cole made a successful escape.'

'And me, what's my next move?' asked Warren.

'You, my old chum, you go into hiding in a safe place. Keep your head down for a couple of days. Grow a beard; get to smell a bit and then you resurface. This is it, Greg, this is what it's all about. So go home, grab your bag, turn off the gas and give you parents a call saying you are going away for a while and the mobile coverage may not be so good. You know the type of stuff. Get back here ASAP before someone recognises you from the news and reports you to the police – now *that* would be ironic.'

'What about my car?'

'Leave it in the compound, we'll have it moved somewhere safe for the duration.'

Warren returned to his home on Delapole Avenue, packed a bag and made sure the services were turned off. The duty call to his mum was duly made and that he'd be in touch when he could.

An hour and a half later, Warren was tucked away in a first floor flat above a ladies' hairdressing salon along Beverley Road, a main road in and out of the city. Access to the flat was by a metal staircase in the rear parking area. Over recent years Beverley Road had been taken over by Eastern European supermarkets, Polish bakers, Lithuanian booze shops and the area was home to speakers of all ethnic communities. The nearer you were to the city the denser the population. The furnished flat was taken on a short term lease, hardly a home from home but adequate for the needs of the operation.

'The fridge is stocked, tea, coffee in the cupboard and there's a bottle of Cole's favourite tipple,' John told him.

Warren picked up the bottle. 'Tequila? I hate tequila,' he put the bottle down on the kitchen table.

'Well you'd better get to like it,' Bob told him, 'your namesake loves the stuff.' He opened his briefcase and took out a familiar looking folder. 'This is your last chance to brush-up; I suggest you take advantage and have one last read through.'

He dropped the folder on the table.

'And take it easy with the tequila, we'll see you in the morning.' John added as they headed for the door.

'Yeah, yeah,' said Warren as he was left alone.

Chapter 4

Warren walked over to the window and pulled the net curtains aside and watched John and Bob drive away. He let the curtain fall back into place and picked up the bottle of tequila. 'In for a penny in for a pound,' he said out loud as he poured himself a generous shot and grimaced at the taste of the fiery liquid. 'Well, this is what you wanted,' he said. 'God knows what sort of mess you've got yourself into,' he sipped again. He sat down on the sofa, glass in hand and clicked the television remote. The early evening news was due to start. He didn't have to wait very long before watching his "own" escape from prison.

> *"Earlier today a vehicle transporting a prisoner to court was involved in a collision with a skip lorry. Although no one was injured in the incident, the accident resulted in the prisoner Raymond Cole absconding from the scene."*

The screen flashed between the damaged vehicles and the surrounding area being searched by uniformed police officers. Then Cole's mugshot flashed up on the screen.

> *"Raymond Cole was being held on remand in Her Majesties Prison Belmarsh, awaiting trial. The reason for his detention has not been disclosed. A Police spokesman urged members of the public not to approach Cole. If anyone should see the fugitive they are to contact the Police immediately. It is believed Cole may be heading for London, and again we stress that under no circumstances should he be approached."*

"Short and sweet". He picked up the tequila and sipped, 'Sod this,' he said, put down the glass and went in search of a can of lager. He turned off the television, sat back on the sofa and spent the rest of the evening concentrating on his "homework" – Raymond Cole. With his iPod on he listened to police interviews that had taken place with Cole. As a child Warren had been good mimicking people's voices, and it wasn't long before he could imitate Cole good enough to fool his casual acquaintances. Warren checked his watch, it was close on 1.30am, he yawned, suddenly feeling tired, everything hit him at once, it had been a long day. The lager and the tequila hadn't helped. The time had come; he could barely keep his eyes focused on the words in the transcripts. 'Enough,' he said and headed for the bathroom then his bed.

At 8.30am next morning Warren was roused from his sleep by a banging on the door. He glanced at his watch on the bedside table, he couldn't believe he'd actually slept in. 'Yeah, yeah, alright I'm coming.' He yelled as he pulled on a pair of jogging pants and stumbled groggily from the bedroom and looked through the door spy-viewer. John and Bob stood on the other side, Bob carrying his briefcase and a loaded paper bag.

John pushed his way past as the door was opened.

'Rough night was it?' He asked when he saw the lager cans on the table.

'If only, I spent most of the night reading up on Cole – again,' Warren said between yawns.

'Glad to hear it. Breakfast,' said Bob, dropping the bag of bacon sandwiches next to the beer cans and placed his briefcase on the floor and took a seat in a well-worn armchair. John sat on the sofa.

'Give me a few minutes while I get a shower will you?' asked Warren.

'Don't bother with the shower or a shave. You're on the run remember?'

'You have a point there,' he replied and went through to the kitchen and filled and turned on the kettle. 'Tea or coffee?' He called from the kitchen; coffee was the order of the morning. 'So, what's the next move?' He asked as he returned carrying three mugs of coffee placing them on a cheap plastic topped coffee table, helped himself to a bacon roll and sat next to John.

John placed a piece of paper next to the coffees.

'Give it a couple of hours and ring this number,' he took a mobile from the briefcase and put it next to the number. 'You make all calls with this phone; someone will be listening in at all times.'

Warren picked up the paper.

'Whose number is it?'

'The number belongs to Mick Conway, he's someone who Cole would be able to rely on in this type of situation. He was in your brief, you *should* know everything about him.'

'Michael Conway, age thirty-eight, overweight, scar below his chin from an incident when he was a kid. His main occupations are drugs and smuggling and robbery – amongst other things. Served eighteen months in Leeds nick, nothing on record for the past five years,' Warren responded, confidently.

Bob raised an eyebrow. 'Excellent. I'm impressed.'

'Do we have an address for him?'

'He has various properties over the city, but resides in a 1920's three-storey town house down the Boulevard.'

'How close are they – Cole and Conway?'

'Business acquaintances in the main, not so much socially. There's virtually no chance you'll be rumbled. If you pull this off you will be home and dry. You report everything, whether you think it's relevant or not.' Warren doubted very much if it was going to be as easy as it sounded. 'They know each other well enough for him to recognise your voice and not think twice about helping. You tell him what's happened and that you'll be in Hull tomorrow, and that you need somewhere to lay low until you can get things sorted.'

'Just like that,' said Warren.

'Just like that. Your cover story will stand up to any scrutiny – as long as *you're* convincing. You'll need some expenses,' John reached into the briefcase once again and produced a large paper envelope and tipped the contents onto the coffee table with the cans and rolls. Six thousand pounds in used notes of various denominations. 'And this should help break the ice.' He handed over a bulging clear plastic bag containing 500 grams of heroin, with a street value of approximately five thousand pounds.

'Bloody hell, where did that come from?' asked Warren.

'Easy come, easy go, confiscated in some drug raid or another.' John made it sound as easy to come by as buying a packet of sweets. 'And there's this,' again reaching into the briefcase. 'Just for insurance.'

It was the very same Sig 17 that Warren had used during his firearms training. Complete with a discreet soft leather shoulder holster. Warren wasn't surprised. He knew it was only a matter of time before he was issued with a firearm.

'This flat is your place of refuge, your sanctuary. Any problem that you can't handle, or you think you've been rumbled, you get out and come here. Ok?' Warren nodded. 'As I said, you only use the mobile you've been issued with, speed dial one and you check-in at least once every twenty-four hours. If by any chance you can't do either, turn yourself in to the nearest police station, give them your real name and rank and say "Suits and Bullets", nothing else, keep your mouth well and truly shut.

'Suits and Bullets?'

'It's just a name thrown up by the computer, but all the same don't knock it,' Bob replied, 'if you have to use it, it will bring a fast response from the people who matter.'

'And who's that?'

'Us.'

Warren's guests stood up to leave. 'Good luck and we'll speak in twenty-four hours.' Both men held out their hands, Warren shook each man's hand in turn. 'From now on you are Cole, don't forget it,' John said as they parted at the flat door.

Warren closed and locked the door behind them. 'Jesus,' he said out loud, 'this is it then.' He picked up the money from the table. *I could always fuck off out of it, head for Spain or somewhere hot*, he thought to himself as he put down the cash. Next was the Sig, he ran his fingers over the cold metal and picked it up, the weapon now felt different – deadly.

Chapter 5

The time had now arrived for Warren to assume the role of Raymond Cole. He stood in front of the bathroom mirror. 'I am Cole, escaped prisoner and an overall badass – badass? What the hell am I talking about?' He laughed out loud at the image in the mirror. Next he picked up the soft leather shoulder holster, slipped it over his shoulders. It felt surprisingly comfortable, this changed when the weight of the Sig was added. He took off the new addition to his wardrobe, walked through to the small lounge and laid it on the coffee table.

It was time to make the phone call. He picked up the mobile and dialled the number written on the paper. His heart pumping adrenaline around his body, excitement – fear? He wasn't sure but every nerve in his body tingled, he felt alive.

Then the phone was picked up at the other end.

'Yeah?'

'Remember me?' he said into the phone.

'Who the fuck should I be remembering?' The voice at the other end demanded to know.

'Cole, Ray Cole…' *I am Cole,* he kept telling himself.

'Fucking hell, you're a quick worker, I was only watching you on the news last night. Where are you?'

'Still down south,' he lied, 'got my head down, but I need to move pretty soon, I fancied coming up north for a while and wondered if you could oblige?' He tried to sound a bit cocky.

'I'm sure it could be arranged… but it won't come cheap,' Conway was quick to add.

'I didn't think it would, I've got to make a bit of a detour and pick up a package. I can be in Hull tomorrow. Can you sort it?'

'No problem pal, give me a ring when you're near the city. It'll be good to get reacquainted.' He ended the call.

'Well that wasn't so bad,' he told himself. His mouth was so dry, nerves, his lips stuck to his teeth. He went into the kitchen, turned on the tap and filled himself a large glass of water and swilled the cold water around his dry mouth. There wasn't much more he could do but wait it out. He still had plenty of food in the fridge and there was the tequila bottle to keep him company. The rest of the day was spent clock watching, watching those crap daytime Australian soaps and the evening thinking, thinking of what might lie ahead of him. He didn't go mad with the tequila, for no better reason than he didn't like the taste and kept with the lager.

Sleep didn't come, it was a night of tossing and turning beneath the duvet, and when he did drift off he'd wake minutes later lathered in a cold sweat. The next morning he was up early feeling totally knackered and longing for a refreshing bath or shower.

He was starting to ming a bit.

Reluctantly, he dressed in the same clothes he'd been wearing for the previous two days. The tension of what lay ahead made his stomach turn somersaults, he hoped a breakfast of toast and coffee would settle the turmoil he felt inside. Then he was back to the clock watching.

At 10am he decided he'd waited long enough. Mobile in one hand, a mug of coffee in the other Warren made the call. 'Me again,' he said into the handset.

'Where are you?' Conway asked.

'Just coming into the city,' he lied.

'How you travelling?'

'I wangled some wheels. Just at the petrol station on the A63, not far from the Humber Bridge.'

Lying was starting to come easy.

'Ok, here are the directions...'

'I'll be ok, been up here a few time just give me an address,' he asked, confidently.

The location he was given wasn't the one he had been expecting. The address Conway gave was for a block of flats on great Thornton Street, not far from the city centre. Warren bided his time and checked his belongings and sorted himself with the essentials a man on the run from the law would have. He also stuffed some cash from the "float" he'd been given in his jacket pocket along with the "sweetener". Apprehensively, he finished off with the soft leather shoulder holster, complete with Sig. The holster no longer felt comfortable, it felt foreign wrapped around his shoulder. It seemed awkward and uncomfortable, but he had the feeling he would soon get used to the feel of the bulge underneath his jacket.

Then he was ready.

Warren had been supplied with a clapped-out looking, green Ford Fiesta, but in reality it was Formula One under the bonnet. Great Thornton Street was on the edge of the city centre, only a ten minute drive away from his safe place. He drove down Beverley Road towards the city centre, a right turn onto Springbank and then a left down Park Street. The road he wanted was directly opposite at the other side of the Anlaby Road junction, Ice House Road. The neighbourhood looked depressed and sorry for itself. The local pub was closed down and boarded up, the shops that were still trading all had metal shutters covering the windows to prevent ram raiding and everywhere was covered in graffiti. The whole place was shabby, it was a shame how it had gone down the nick.

Warren drove down Ice House Road and pulled into the kerb side, took a few deep breaths to compose himself, then put the car into gear and drove the 100 metres to his final destination. He pulled up in a concrete parking area of a thirteen-storey block of council flats bearing the grand name of Hawthorn House. The place was littered with beer cans, takeaway wrappers. A group of dubious looking youths stood by the entrance door drinking cans of strong cider and passing around what looked like a spliff. He double-checked the car was locked and confidently strode towards the group, no one approached or said anything, just gave him the evil eye as he passed. He was glad the car wasn't much to look at; there was less chance of it getting nicked.

The flat Warren wanted was on the third floor, which was just as well as the lift had a sign stuck to the doors 'Out of Order'. He trundled up the concrete stairwell stepping over more takeaway wrappers and beer cans, the whole place smelled of piss. Warren was looking for number fifteen; he found it directly opposite the stairwell. The door of number fifteen was reinforced with a sheet of battle scarred steel plate, a spyhole at head height looked straight out into the hallway. He stood for a moment checking down the corridor, looking both ways, then banged on the metal with his fist, he had a feeling he was being scrutinised through the spyhole. Click – click, scuff, the locks were unlocked and the deadlocks grated as they were slid free. The door was opened by a scruffy-looking youth wearing combat trousers, a well-worn hoody and his face covered in tats and piercings, a face that only a drunken mother could love. He stood to one side to let Warren pass. He nodded to the youth and walked down the long hallway towards the open door at the far end. His first impression was one of surprise, it looked ok – clean and tidy, not the doss house he was expecting.

'Man, it's good to see your black arse again,' Conway said as he eased his large frame out of a leather armchair and walked across the room towards Warren, arm outstretched and pumped Warren's hand in a vice like grip.

Warren's Mum was as white as driven snow with blonde hair and blue eyes and came from North London, his Dad was West Indian from Jamaica, and as black as night. Warren – he was somewhere in between, edging more towards the darker side, a strange combination if you took into account his pale blue eyes.

'And you Mick,' he said, 'it's been quite a while.'

Conway was shorter than he appeared on the videos Warren had watched, and fatter. It was difficult to conceive that this man had his fingers in just about all the pies that mattered, not referring to all the pies he must have eaten.

'Come in mate, make yourself at home,' Conway returned to his chair. Warren cleared some motoring magazines of the leather sofa and sat.

He dropped his rucksack on the floor beside him. 'Cop for this,' Conway passed over a can of lager.

Warren was grateful. Nerves had dried his mouth completely.

'Cheers,' he sipped, 'I was ready for that.'

'Well?' he asked.

'Well what?'

'The great escape, what else? I want to know how you sorted it. Like Houdini this fella,' he said, turning to the youth. 'Fucking Houdini, you could learn a lot from him.' He settled back in his chair and swigged from the can and waited.

Warren told him the story, not the tale portrayed on the television, one with more than a few embellishments. A tale of "inside corruption", of messages passed via one of the screws on the payroll, how he'd organised a team from Southern Ireland to take out the Prison van and sort him out with a motor.

'Why use a team of Paddies?

'Simple, I didn't want to use anyone who might be associated with me. These lads flew into Heathrow from Dublin, did the job and then were on the next flight back via Manchester Airport.'

'I'm impressed, man. You sorted all that from inside?'

'Easy if you find a screw up to his neck in debt and desperate for some readies, know what I mean.'

The lying was coming easier.

'So, Ray, what can I do for you beside the obvious?'

'First off I need a place to get my head down for a while until things settle down a bit. Secondly, money doesn't last forever, my assets have been seized. Once I've got some cash together I'm away.' Sounding good, he was pleased.

'You skint then?'

'Not skint, but you know what it's like, I've got a bit of a stash but as I said it won't last forever.'

Conway leaned forward in his chair. 'What's in it for me if I help get you sorted?'

So much for honour amongst thieves, thought Warren. He reached down to the backpack on the floor beside him, opened it and took out the package and threw it over.

'Here's a down payment.'

'Sweet. Welcome to your new home, fella,' Conway said smugly as he caught the plastic bag of class 'A'.

The next half an hour tested Warren to the limit, stories of old, mutual acquaintances and deals gone down. His homework stood him in good stead and he managed to hold his own. It was a relief when the youth who had so far been sat quiet taking it all in, looked at his watch, and nodded his head towards the door.

'Got to be on me way Ray, somewhere to be. This is your home for as long as you need it,' he said tossing the package of class 'A' to the tat covered scally. 'Give me your mobile,' Warren passed it over and Conway proceeded to key in a number. 'If you need anything give me a call on this number,' he passed back the mobile. 'Ok? And don't forget, anything you want, women, boys, just let me know.'

'Cheers Mick, I appreciate the help. And don't forget about the other business.'

'No problem pal I'll keep you in mind, I'll be in touch.' Warren was glad to see Conway waddle his fat frame down the hallway.

'Jimbo, here will get you some new clobber and supplies and drop them off later,' the tattooed youth turned, half smiled and gave Warren the keys to the flat.

'Jimbo,' Warren called after them. Jimbo turned. 'Don't forget a bottle of tequila.'

Then they were gone.

Warren shut the door and locked it, then he gave the biggest sigh of his life as leaned against the closed door. The back of his shirt was soaked with sweat. He was desperate to quench his nervous thirst. He went through to the kitchen and sure enough the fridge was well stocked with Carlsberg Export. Standing in the kitchen, Warren held out the arm holding the can and it was shaking.

'Thank fuck that's over,' he said out loud, as he tried to control the shakes.

After taking a few deep breaths he managed to get himself together. Next, he did a quick exploration of the flat. There were two bedrooms, one was quite well furnished: double bed, chest of drawers, wardrobe and bedside cabinet and looked comfortable, even the decorating was passable. On the other hand, the smaller of the two was obviously used for storage. If he had been a smoker he'd never have wanted for contraband tobacco for the rest of his life. The bathroom wasn't too bad, although Warren thought it might benefit from a bottle of bleach. The sitting room was snug, cosy his Mum would have called it, with the leather sofa and chair, dining table and of course a flat screen television, obviously. He did a quick search through the oak sideboard and cupboards, also a "sweep", just in case there was any listening devices. Nothing.

It was time to make the call.

Chapter 6

John was the first in the office, he was always the early bird, first in the office and the last to leave. A few minutes later his colleague walked in bearing two takeaway cups of Costa coffee.

'Have a good night?' Bob asked as he set down the cardboard cups and dropped into a chair.

'Not so good, I'll sleep better when we've had a call. Cheers,' he said holding up the cardboard cup, 'thanks.'

'So no contact yet?'

'No not so far.'

'Once he's established himself things will take their own course and settle down – only a matter of time.'

'True, no point worrying until we hear something.'

Then as if on cue the phone rang. There was only one person who would call on that particular number.

'Gemmell Strategies.'

'Warren here,' Warren said and waited for a reply.

'Greg, it's good to hear from you.' It sounded like John's voice. 'How did the meeting go?'

'The meeting went fine, it's my nerves that are shot.'

'Any problems?'

'None, looks like we're in. I'm in a flat on Great Thornton Street.'

'Yes we know, there's a GPS tracker in your vehicle.'

'Of course there is – the flat number is fifteen.'

'Thank you Greg, keep in touch.' He hung up, a short and maybe not so sweet conversation. John sat back in his swivel chair, relieved Warren had made contact. With his arms folded behind his head he visibly relaxed.

'So, are you feeling better?' asked Bob.

'Marginally,' he said smiling. 'I think it's time to make the call.'

'Shall I do the honours?'

Bob didn't wait for a reply. He walked over and sat behind his own desk, picked up his mobile from the desk and tapped in a series of numbers. The call was answered almost straightaway.

'Today would be good, let me know when the obstacle has been removed,' he said into the handset and hung up.

'First stage complete, onwards and upwards,' John picked up his coffee. 'Cheers,' he said once more, this time gesturing with the cardboard cup.

Chapter 7

Warren checked out the kitchen, thankfully there was something other than lager in the fridge, a pack of bacon and half a dozen eggs, plenty to satisfy his retuning appetite until the lad came back with supplies. He made himself a fry-up and waited.

A couple of hours or so later there was a hammering on the flat door, Warren looked through the viewer, it was Jimbo loaded up with paper carrier bags.

'Bloody hell Jimbo, you bought the shop?' The lad smiled and shrugged his shoulders.

He took the bags off Jimbo, tipped them onto the table and examined the contents.

'Didn't know what size to get, so I got large in everything,' said Jimbo as he watched.

Warren thought it looked like he'd bought enough provisions to keep him going for a week, along with a selection of new clothes from Primarni. Not his usual choice of clothing store, but perfectly in line with what Cole would wear, cheap underwear, jeans, T-shirts and jumpers and a new zip-up hoody jacket.

'Not forgetting this,' he said producing a bottle of tequila from a separate bag.

'Top man,' Warren said accepting the bottle. 'Fancy one?' He didn't think Jimbo would refuse, and it was also an opportunity for him to drop in some sly questions. 'Grab some glasses from the kitchen.' Warren settled into Conway's leather chair while Jimbo poured out two generous tots. 'Cheers, mate,' he said raising the glass and sipping. 'You worked for Mick very long?'

Simple enough question Warren thought.

'Two years, on and off.'

'And what is it you do for him?'

'This and that.'

Warren concluded it was going to be hard work, he doubted he'd get very much out of him. Not yet any way, he had to win his trust.

'Like what?'

'What's with all the questions?'

He was a suspicious bugger, his eyes narrowed as he spoke.

'Just trying to make conversation. I've spent the last few weeks on remand, listening to a load of cons bragging about what they have and haven't done. Just wanted a proper conversation with someone who hasn't got a chip on their shoulder.'

'Fair enough I suppose. I just do whatever he asks, courier work mainly – you know collections and delivery.'

'So we might get the chance to work together. I'll look forward to it,' he lied.

'Anyway, I've got to make a move, places to be.' Jimbo stood to leave and downed the remaining tequila from the glass. 'Be seeing ya.'

'Thanks for the supplies,' Warren said holding up his glass as he watched him leave. Then Warren immediately followed him and slid the dead bolts in to place. There was nothing more to do than play the waiting game. It was time for the long-awaited shower and a change of clothes.

Chapter 8

Life for Raymond Cole, the *real* Raymond Cole was not exactly one of luxury. After all he *was* being held on 'remand' in the segregation block of HMP Belmarsh, and life wasn't meant to be pleasant, but he was the first to admit he'd had worse HMP accommodation. Cole's gripe was that he couldn't understand why he was being held in 'special segregation' without any explanation. He was a 'real' criminal why should they hold him on the same wing as the paedophiles, rapists and perverts?

Cole hated nonces.

All in all, Cole wasn't expecting to be incarcerated for very long, after all, he hadn't been charged. He had over the years been a frequent short stay visitor to Her Majesty's establishments, and it was an easy life on the segregation wing. If the monotony didn't get to you the boredom did, especially now as the issue of daily newspapers had stopped, strangely enough coinciding with his non-existent 'escape'. Two days previous, there had been uproar amongst the inmates, with no explanation given every television and radio on the wing had been removed. When Cole asked what was going on, he was told 'mind your own fucking business' if he didn't want to spend time in solitary.

Cole kept himself to himself, he didn't want or encourage conversations with the any of the nonces, after all he was a *proper* criminal not some kiddie fiddler. When approached by a fellow inmate he made his feeling very clear – verbally and occasionally by resorting to physical violence. Only the previous week a nonce with a history of child rape and murder had tried to play the big man, bragging about his heinous deeds to anyone who would listen.

Cole had had enough of the heinous talk and put him in the prison infirmary laid on his front for two days having the wound in his arse taken care of. Needless to say, he made himself unpopular amongst his peers; any one of them would 'top' him given the opportunity.

Lunchtime came around, Cole picked up a tray along with the obligatory plastic cutlery and joined the queue in the canteen. He collected his barely edible meal, and as usual he preferred his own company and returned to his cell. He sat on the edge of his bed poking and prodding at the slop on the tray when Peter Price, the nonce he'd had a run-in with two days previous entered his cell. He stood leaning on the doorframe, like a man on a mission.

'What the fuck do you want, twat?'

'Not *your* arse that's for sure.' Price retorted, still bearing the battle scars of their previous encounter, namely twelve stitches in the cheek of his arse.

'How is your arse by the way?' asked Cole.

'Wanker,' he said as he walked further in to the cell, his right hand behind his back.

'Just fuck off back under your rock.' Cole put his tray beside him on the bed and stood up. 'Hear me nonce? Just piss off, if you don't I'm telling you your face will match your arse.' Cole had stuck a broken plastic dinner knife into Price's arse cheek and gouged out a chunk of flesh.

Price stepped forward; his right arm came from behind his back holding a nine-inch Perspex shiv sharpened to a point. He took one step further forward into the cell and he thrust the shiv into Cole, just below the ribs with an upward twist. Cole didn't have time to defend himself as the shiv was deliberately snapped, leaving the blade buried deep inside his body. It was over in seconds.

Cole dropped to his knees, grasping his wound, blood seeped through his fingers, he couldn't comprehend what had just happened.

'Now who's a twat?' He heard the nonce say, as Price left leaving him doubled over in a pool of crimson.

Price walked out of the cell onto the landing and passed the shiv handle to the screw standing by the side of the door, and then calmly walked through the open gateway to his own wing. Price had nothing to lose, he was already serving four life sentences, and he knew he was never going to leave prison alive. So what if he was convicted of killing Cole? They couldn't do anything else to him. No words were spoken between Price and the screw. The prison guard calmly put the handle in his pocket and walked to the toilets and then dropped what was left of the Perspex shiv in the floor drain, washed his hands and made a phone call on his mobile. 'It's done,' was all he said, ended the call. He removed the

SIM card from the mobile, snapped it in half and sent it to join the shiv in the drain.

He then went back to Cole's cell and pressed the panic button.

Chapter 9

Holed up in the flat with only the television for company, Warren was starting to get cabin fever. After forty-eight hours he was unwisely considering having a walk in the fresh air.

Then contact.

As they had arranged, Conway gave two rings on the mobile before he banged on the flat door.

'Raymondo,' he shouted from out in the hallway.

The dead bolts grated as Warren slid them open. Conway and his sidekick Jimbo followed him back into the lounge.

'About time, I thought you'd forgotten about me, I've been talking to myself since Jimbo left.'

'Yeah well, business, you know what it's like. Some of that tequila left? Don't really matter.' Jimbo passed over a bottle he'd been carrying.

'Came prepared,' he held up a bottle of single malt. 'This is more my tipple,' he said as he made straight for the glasses. 'Want one?' He called from the kitchen. He didn't wait for an answer and came back juggling three fat stubby glasses.

'Cheers,' Warren said taking the offered glass.

Compared to the tequila, the malt tasted like liquid heaven. Conway dropped down onto the sofa, while Jimbo pulled out a straight back chair. It was obvious Conway had already had a drink or three, at least.

'Now here's the thing, since you turned up I've been doing some thinking and I've got a deal to put to you. By the way, Bernie sends his regards.'

Warren searched his memory bank trying to remember the name. Nothing he couldn't remember a Bernie.

'Yeah well, can't say I did that much business with him. Bit of a tosser if I remember rightly. So what's this deal you want to put to me?' Swiftly changing the subject.

'Hang on a minute Ray, let's not rush things. Jimbo, go grab us some cans to go with the Scotch.'

Warren sat patiently, he guessed he wasn't going to like Conway's latest proposal. Jimbo did as he was told and went through to Warren's kitchen, it wasn't as if he didn't know where things were kept, and returned with three cans of Export lager.

'Come on Mick, don't have me sitting here all day.' Warren said as Jimbo passed him a can.

'Well, after your tale about the "great escape" I got to thinking, what if we pinched the idea?'

'What do you mean pinched the idea?'

'I mean we knock off a security van.'

'It's been done before Mick, it's not very original.'

'Maybe, but not for a good few years, it worked for you or you wouldn't be sitting here now,' he pulled the tab on the can and took a sip. 'I'm thinking along the lines of a cash in transit van, you know all loaded up after doing a day's collections.'

'Bloody hell Mick, that'll take some setting up.' Warren was right, he didn't like the way things were heading.

'Not if we keep things simple, it's just a case of knowing where to make the hit. All I say is keep an open mind while I work out some details.'

'What would be my cut in all this?'

'Eighty – twenty split.'

'Pull the other one Mick – it plays Birdie Song! Fifty – fifty.'

'Now who's taking the piss! Sixty – forty, final offer.'

'That'll do nicely thank you very much, cheers. But it will have to be a bloody good plan, I don't want to end up back behind bars.'

'Good man, knew I'd be able to rely on you,' he held up the can in a mock salute. 'Cheers.'

None of this was going the way Warren expected it to. He thought the operation would just involve intelligence gathering, ok, maybe he would have to get involved in some underhand deals, but robbing an armoured security van was *not* something he wanted any part of.

'So, we put that on the back burner for a bit, in the meantime I have a bit of work to put your way, still interested Raymondo?'

He was all but slurring his words.

'Like I said, my stash won't keep me in luxuries forever.' This was the opening he had been waiting for, he just wasn't expecting it too soon. 'A mate of mine wants a favour.'

'Not the kind of favour that involves killing anyone I hope?'
Laughs all around.

'Na, nothing too taxing. Jimbo here is overseeing an exchange, a wagon-load of booze for a large package of "H".

'How large a package?'

Warren sipped the malt. It was good.

'Fifty grand, thereabouts.'

Conway said it without even blinking.

'Which way is the swap?'

'Well, it's like this – I've arranged for a lorry full of export Black Label Whisky to be knocked off on the A1. My lads deliver it to the meet, Jimbo here hands the lorry over in exchange for the "H". All you have to do is watch his back. Easy, a piece of piss.'

'When's this happening?' Warren asked casually.

'Can't tell you that man, not until I know you're in.'

'I'm just being on the cagey side Mick; after all I *am* on the run, and its early days yet I'm supposed to be keeping my head down and not going out the way to get my collar felt.'

'You're a fucking worrier that's what you are. Who the fuck is going to be looking for you up here in this shit hole? The cops will be concentrating down South,' he said convincingly.

'Suppose you're right, ok, how much is in it for me?'

'Besides your bed and breakfast? There'll be a good drink in it. Like I said, it's a piece of piss, what can go wrong?' *If only you knew*, thought Warren. 'You in or what?'

'Yeah, what have I got to lose beside my liberty? I'm in. Jimbo fill the glasses, I'll have tequila not this muck.' Warren held up the fat glass tumbler of delicious malt as if it was dishwater. He thought it wise to keep to the script. The whisky and tequila kept flowing, well the whisky did. Warren took his slowly adding a drop of water to the tequila when he had the chance.

'You hungry Ray?'

'Starving, I could eat a scabby horse.' Warren was genuinely seriously hungry.

'Jimbo get yourself down to *Billie's Plaice* and get us three large portions.'

Jimbo didn't argue and was dispatched to fetch fish and chips from the local chippie. Alone with Conway, Warren thought maybe this was his opportunity to glean some information.

'Seems a good lad,' he said, 'once you get past the tats and piercings. Just goes to prove appearances are deceptive. He worked for you long?'

'Aye, he's not a bad lad, been with me... must be a couple of years now.'

'You trust him?' Warren sat sprawled, legs out in front trying to look and act half-pissed.

'Yep, he may be young but I knew his old man before he topped himself. Told his mam I'd keep an eye on him.'

'What happened?'

'The Big C, too many fags. He decided he didn't want to carry on with the treatment and bloody hung himself. It was the lad who found him, hanging from the banister by his dressing gown cord.'

'Jesus, rough, how did the lad take it?'

'He was devastated, what with his mam having the early onset of dementia. I told her not to worry and I'd look after him.'

'Where's his mam now?'

'Some crappy council run nursing home.'

The conversation was beginning to lean towards the morbid side, Warren changed tack.

'Seen much of Jim Douglas, lately?' he asked conjuring up one of the names from his homework.

'Funny you should ask, I was on the blower to him yesterday discussing the possibility of a future deal. We did a bit of business together a couple of months back, he was bringing some bodies across from Holland.'

'He's stepped it up a bit, I thought he was more into a bit of baccy and booze,' Warren nodded his head towards the spare room, 'didn't know he was into the serious stuff.'

'Yeah well, supply and demand. Seems we might be on again pretty soon if you're interested?'

'Hell fire Mick, one job at a time,' Warren joked, 'don't want my collar felt too soon. Know what I mean?' They both laughed.

Jimbo came back with their fish suppers, along with more booze, lager this time. Warren had forgotten how good fish and chips tasted when eaten out of the paper wrapping.

'Nice fish this,' he said as he sucked the grease from his fingers.

'Well it's more who you know, know what I mean?' he tapped the side of his nose with his finger. ''Cos they know if they sell me

or my lad any crap that they can't fry fish with deep fried fingers.'
They both creased up laughing. Warren believed every word he'd
said.

The lorry full of booze was to be "hijacked" at the Peterborough
Services on the A1M, on its way to Dover. The term "hijacked"
was an exaggeration, as the driver of the truck was aware of what
was going to happen. He was to leave his truck, grab a coffee and
go to the gents. When he returned the vehicle would be gone.
What the driver didn't know was while he was in the gents he was
to receive a nasty tap on the head to help keep things realistic. The
exchange was to be made the same day, with a crew from
Newcastle at the Goole Lorry Park, thirty miles west of Hull. It
turned out Warren's role was as the Watcher, just to keep his eye
on things and pull Jimbo out if he suspected anything untoward.

Eventually goodnights were said, Warren's nerves were shot,
he'd been swapping battle stories with Conway for what seemed
like hours.

Chapter 10

Even though he thought he'd taken it easy with the booze, Warren's head throbbed when he woke the next morning. He didn't feel too good. This coupled with the fact the flat smelled of stale booze and old greasy fish and chips didn't help. Unfortunately, the hot water boiler was on the blink and a quick cold shower shocked some life into him. *He'd have to tell the landlord,* he joked to himself. Warren made himself some coffee and sat mulling over the events of past days and weeks. A hell of a lot had happened and he didn't know where it was going. A quick tidy of the flat was called for, he dumped the cans and chip wrappers down the communal rubbish chute, and then it was time to make the call.

Watching was one thing, but taking part in a full blown armed robbery was a different proposition all together, one which he really didn't want to be a part of. He'd signed up for some excitement and it looked like he was going to get his share. He gave it half an hour to be sure Conway or Jimbo wouldn't turn up mid-call, then pressed speed dial one.

'Greg, an unscheduled call, I take it there are developments?' The voice belonged to John.

'Things are starting to move.'

'Already… I am surprised, tell me more.' For the benefit of John, Bob put the call on speaker phone.

'There's to be an exchange made, a wagon load of booze for a substantial amount of class 'A'.'

'And when is this to take place?'

'The exchange is later today – early evening.'

'And you're happy to take part, so soon after making contact?'

'The job's obviously been set up for ages. I reckon he's sussing me out, a test.'

'And your role?'

'Watcher, I'm to look after Conway's lad's back when the exchange takes place. They call him Jimbo, don't know his real name at this stage.'

'You have the details?'

Warren told him as much as he knew.

'How are you going to play this – you going to intervene?' He asked.

'Not this time, everything will go as planned without any interference from outside. Just keep us in the loop.'

'Before you hang up, he's after putting a team together to rob a Securicash van.'

'You have any details?'

'Not yet, still in the planning stage.'

'Righto, let us know when you have more information.'

'Hang on I haven't finished yet. What's your take on an armed robbery?'

'How soon is this to take place?'

'Imminent, that's all I can say.'

'I think maybe we should discuss this in person, how soon can you be at your safe place?'

'As soon as you like, I need some guidance.'

'Be there this evening.' The line was disconnected.

Chapter 11

It was Warren's first visit to the Beverley Road flat since making contact with Conway. The place felt cold, unlived-in, he turned on the gas fire and waited. He didn't have to wait long before there was a knock on the door, he checked the door viewer, the distorted faces of John and Bob looked back.

He unlocked the door and let them in. 'Good to see you Greg,' Bob said as they entered.

'John tells me you're seeking advice?'

'You could say that. Conway wants to rope me into an armed assault on a cash in transit van – that's all,'

'I don't think we can allow that to happen,' John said as he sat on a straight back dining chair. 'Have you made coffee?'

'Sorry for being an inhospitable host, but making you a brew was the last thing on my mind,' he said sarcastically as he went through to the kitchen, filled and turned on the kettle.

'Instant will be fine,' John called back.

'Bloody good, that's all there is!'

Bob and John exchanged smiles.

'Coffee,' Warren placed three mugs down on the coffee table.'

'Thanks very much Greg, I can't function without my caffeine. Now, how much do you know about the operation?'

Warren sat down on the settee, leaning forward, forearms on his knees nursing his coffee mug in both hands. 'At this moment very little, Conway reckons on basing the hit on my *escape*,

'Look how are we going to play this, it isn't as if I can refuse, it's something the "real" Cole wouldn't blink an eyelid at.'

'As things stand there's little we can do until you get confirmation of how and when this will happen.'

'So that's it then?'

'Afraid so Greg,' they stood up to leave. 'Once you have more details then we can act accordingly.'

Bob and John abruptly left leaving Warren feeling out of his depth, and thinking it wasn't supposed to be like this.

Chapter 12

Forty-eight hours after making contact and Warren was in it up to his neck. If truth was known, he was not a happy bloke, not one little bit – but what could he do about it? Sod all. Jimbo was picking him up at five o'clock, they reckoned that would give them plenty of time to get to the meet and check things out. Warren took advantage of the down time to reacquaint himself with the Sig, even though he hadn't discharged the weapon since the firing range, he thought a strip down and clean couldn't hurt. After all, best be prepared.

With still two hours to kill before Jimbo was picking him up, Warren took advantage of the down time and went through to the bedroom and lay on top of the duvet, staring up at the ceiling. Sleep didn't come easy. He kept going over the *what ifs* until eventually he nodded off and managed an hour or so before waking up feeling like crap. A quick cold shower helped put some of the life back into him, followed by some strong black coffee.

Warren's mobile rang twice and then there was a banging at the door, he checked the security viewer in the door. It was Jimbo. Sliding the bolts on the door was a knack, you had to ease them around a bit and give them a firm tug.

'Bang on time mate,' he said as he walked in, 'go through.'

'Shit,' he cursed himself as they walked into the living room. He'd left the Sig on the table in full view.

'For fuck's sake man, that's one serious shooter.'

Jimbo headed straight for the Sig.

'I'd prefer it if you didn't,' said Warren grabbing Jimbo's wrist firmly as his hand reached out. 'Nothing personal.'

'Whatever.' He shrugged his shoulders. 'You ready?'

'Just finish dressing, then we're away.'

It was too late now to pull out; even if he wanted too. He put on the shoulder holster complete with Sig and fastened the safety catch, all nicely concealed beneath his jacket. If he'd had the option he would have preferred to leave the weapon in the flat, but he would have put money on that he might not be the only one with a set of keys.

Watching Jimbo eyeing up the holster beneath his jacket, it looked as if he'd found some respect.

'Right then mate, let's get a shift on,' Warren said slamming the door behind them. They took the evil smelling concrete stairs two at a time to the car park. The only vehicle besides Warren's Fiesta was a dark blue Audi 4x4. 'This Mick's motor?'

'One of 'em, not too flashy but makes a statement. Right?' He sounded proud.

'Does that alright Jimbo.' Then he noticed another body sat in the rear seats. He looked to be in his mid-twenties, hard face with a nice curved scar running from his left eyebrow to his lip, shaved head and dressed in denim. 'Who the fuck is this? Mick never said anything about a passenger.'

'Who the fuck you calling a passenger?' Scar face answered back.

'Come on Ray, get real, this is Billybob. You didn't think I was doing this on me own?' He kept his mouth shut. It made sense even if Warren didn't like the look of him. If Conway rated the bloke he was bound to be good at whatever he was employed for.

'What sort of bleedin' name is Billybob?' Warren laughed as he said it, keeping up the appearance of the hard man.

'You'll be laughing out of the other side of your fucking face in a minute,' Billybob said.

'Like you did? No offence meant.'

Warren leaned into the back of the vehicle, offering his hand.

'Fuck off,' he turned to look out of the window.

'Please yourself…Billybob,' he said keeping a straight face. Jimbo and Billybob he thought, what sort of crew was this?

Jimbo drove the Audi out of the tower block parking area and headed for the A63, the Clive Sullivan Way that followed the banks of the River Humber, under the Humber Bridge, onto the M62 and Goole, some thirty miles west.

'You used it then?' Jimbo asked.

'Used what?' Warren asked.

'The shooter.'

'When there wasn't any other option,' he lied.

'Cool'.

'What you got? asked Billybob.

'Sig P226.'

'Pass it here then,' he said leaning between the front seats.

'Fuck off, hillbilly.' At least it produced a laugh out of Jimbo. Billybob kept quiet and sat back in his seat. 'Jimbo, you had dealings with this team before?'

'Once or twice. Should be three of them, the bloke we'll be dealing with is one of their top dogs, Jack Spriggs, hard bastard.'

That was a name that wasn't in Warren's portfolio.

'Who runs the show?'

'Fucked if I know, just do as I'm told.'

It took just over half an hour to get to Goole. The lorry park wasn't too far away from the docks. The small team did a quick drive past to get the lay of the land, a two storey building was to the left of the entrance – the café and drivers accommodation on the second floor. The shower block was adjacent. Jimbo turned the vehicle around and pulled up a couple of hundred metres short of the entrance and let Warren out. It was a big place, enough room for at least fifty rigs. The whole place was surrounded by a high wire-mesh security fence.

Posters and signs fixed to the fence claimed high security. Warren could see a couple of cameras high on poles, from the loose dangling electric feed wires he doubted very much that they worked. Nevertheless he made a mental note to keep out of their view as much as possible. All in all, the wire mesh surrounding the park was totally inadequate for any real security. Warren checked no one was looking and grabbed a flapping wire panel. After a couple of tugs it was loose enough to crawl under. He dropped to his knees and eased his body under the wire.

Commercial transport of all kind and nationalities were represented, articulated trucks from Poland, panel vans from Belgium and curtain sided vehicles from the UK, everything from everywhere. Warren walked around the inside of the perimeter, between, and in and out of the parked vehicles looking for anyone or anything a bit suss. Everything looked fine. He picked up the 4x4 again near the back fence, tucked out of view between a container truck and freezer lorry, well away from the café and drivers shower block.

The trimming knife in Warren's pocket came in handy. He slit the plastic sheeting on a curtain-sided lorry and climbed in. He couldn't see anyone nicking this one, it was full of bottles of bleach and drain cleaner, through the slit he had a pretty good view of the area. Jimbo and the hillbilly sat and waited in the car. Ten minutes later a big black Mercedes drove down the gravel road and stopped alongside the Audi. One big guy climbed out of the Mercedes, looked around and then walked around to the driver's side of the Audi. Warren watched as Jimbo opened the car window. The guy stuck his head in and said something. The other two climbed out of the Mercedes and stood around the passenger side, big fellas. Warren felt he really needed to be in on this, Watcher or no Watcher. He jumped down from the truck and casually made his way over. As soon as he was within earshot the two passengers from the Mercedes blocked his way. They nearly blocked out the early evening sun they were so big. As Warren approached the four-wheel drive the flat of a hand knocked the breath out of him.

'Whoa – man, where the fuck do you think you're going?'

Then he must have felt the Sig under Warren's jacket. He'd never seen such a big bloke react so fast in all his life. He reached around the back of his trouser waistband and produced his own Sig, then stuck the barrel in Warren's chest. He put his hands up. *Keep cool, smile at the bad guy.*

'It's ok, Carl, he's with us,' Jimbo told him.

The hillbilly was laughing his head off at Warren's predicament.

'What do you think you're doing?' Jimbo asked as he walked over.

'Just came over to make sure things were going ok.'

Before Jimbo had a chance to have a go at him, Top Dog, the first guy to get out of the Mercedes walked around towards Warren.

'And you are?'

'Cole, Ray Cole you might have seen me on the television?' Warren did a big cheesy grin. 'And you are?'

'I'm the fucker you don't want to mess with. Do I know you?'

Billybob was excited as a young kid. 'This is the bloke who just escaped from Belmarsh, he's a mate of Mick's.'

'Thought you looked familiar – Jack Spriggs,' he said holding out his hand, 'good to meet you, Cole.'

'Likewise.'

Spriggs took a hold of Warren's hand and shook, giving him the evil eye while he did.

Jimbo gave Billybob one of those *I wish you'd keep your gob shut type of looks,* and shook his head in dismay. Before they had a chance to get further acquainted, a sixteen wheel articulated lorry drove around the circular gravel road towards the little group.

'This is us,' Jimbo said as the lorry came to a stop 10 metres or so away, facing the park entrance. The driver and his mate stayed in the vehicle.

Nice, thought Warren, ready to take off if things went pear shaped.

The bloke who climbed down from the passenger side of the lorry actually looked *normal,* no bulging muscles, clean shaven and tat free. The driver remained in the cab.

'Any problems? Asked Jimbo as he walked over.

'Na, all went well. Done in ten minutes, changed the licence plates and away.'

'And the driver?'

'Probably tucked up in a hospital bed by now chatting up the nurses.' Obviously this brought a few laughs, still Warren reckoned the injured driver was well paid for the inconvenience.

'Let's go and have a look at what we've got.' Spriggs led the way to the rear of the vehicle. The security seal on the rear doors was snapped and the doors opened. 'Eureka,' Spriggs said as he saw boxes of Black Label Whisky piled high. 'Looks like we've got a deal Jimbo, man.'

He nodded to one of his tame henchmen who headed back to the Mercedes and opened the boot, returning with a leather briefcase. The case was placed on the bonnet of the Audi. Spriggs released the latches and there it was, two big fat packages of "H".

'Don't mind if I test the product do you?' Jimbo didn't wait for an answer, he took a pen knife from his pocket and made a tiny slit, dipped his finger into the powder and then rubbed the substance on his gums. 'Sweet,' was all he said and closed the case.

Jimbo gave the lorry's driver a nod. He climbed down from the cab, walked over to where Spriggs was standing and passed over the keys, then he and his mate walked away into the sunset. Job done.

'Nice doing business with you Jimbo,' Spriggs said as he passed on the lorry keys to one of his men. 'Might see you again in the future Cole – stay out of trouble.' With that Spriggs and his colleague were back in the Mercedes and crunching gravel on the way back to Geordie land. The lorry load of booze following.

'What the fuck was all that about? You were supposed to be the Watcher – you know, keep out of the way and *watch?*'

'Come on Jimbo, I didn't like the look of Spriggs blokes, thought there might be a bit of aggro,' Warren said attempting to smooth the way.

'We've done business with Spriggs plenty of times in the past and there's never been any bother.' Hillbilly was loving it, seeing Warren get a bollocking. He shrugged his shoulders. 'Next time just do as you're supposed to. Ok?'

'Whatever you say Jimbo – whatever you say.' Warren said through gritted teeth to emphasis he was no push over. 'And you, just keep out of my bleedin' face,' he told Billybob.

'I'll give Mick a call, he'll be wanting to know what's what.'

Jimbo walked away, stood by the Audi and took his mobile out. Warren could see the conversation was animated by the way he kept glancing in his direction every couple of seconds. He hoped he hadn't blown it.

Once they were back in the Audi, things returned to normal. The trip back to Hull was all talk of how well the deal had gone and how pleased Conway was going to be. Warren supposed he would be, he'd made a shed load of money for staying at home.

Chapter 13

'Gemmell Strategies.'

It was Bob, Warren was getting good at the voice recognition.

'It's me.'

'Of course it is, how did it go?'

'As planned, the goods were delivered and the exchange went well without any hitches.'

'And the faces?'

'There was a new one on Conway's team – young bloke, shaved head, skinny but tough looking and he has a curved scar on the left side of his face running from eyebrow to mouth. Goes by the name of Billybob.'

'Did I hear correctly?'

'Yes you did, Billybob, haven't a clue what his real name is. The exchange was with three of a Newcastle team, again they were not in the portfolio. Does the name Jack Spriggs mean anything?'

'Not immediately, leave it with me and I'll get back to you. In future see if you can get a photograph of any of his colleagues you cannot identify. Goodnight, Raymond.'

As if the thought hadn't occurred to Warren, it was easier said than done, it's not as if you can say hold it there, smile while I take your pic! That was the phone call out of the way, now he had to wait and see if he was to get a bollocking from Conway.

It never came. Warren was seriously beginning to wonder if he'd put the operation in jeopardy.

In the front room of Conway's home down the Boulevard, he sat in an expensive easy chair nursing a lead crystal glass of single malt, listening to the evening's events.

Jimbo was letting it be known he wasn't happy with the new member of the team. 'I'm telling you Mick, he's a fucking liability. He came waltzing in on the action as if it was his operation.' He took out his tobacco tin, removed a paper from the packet and stuck it to his bottom lip. 'The bloke's a fucking nut job, that's what he is,' the paper quivered as he spoke.

'Come on Jimbo, he's a top man, he knows the game. He wouldn't have shown himself if he didn't think it was necessary.'

Jimbo continued rolling his smoke, flipped his lighter and lit up.

'You never saw him Mick…' Billybob tried to add his tuppence worth but was cut off before he could finish.

'And what's it got to do with you, fuckwit? Fuck all that's what! You're just the hired help so keep your fucking neb out and your gob shut.' Conway didn't mince his words.

'Just sayin' that's all.'

'Well fucking don't, ok?'

'You've got to have a word with him Mick,' Jimbo sucked on the soggy roll-up.

'I will Jimbo, I will. What you've got to remember, Cole is a very handy bloke, know what I mean? You said yourself he has a serious shooter, and I know for a fact he isn't afraid to use it.

'Yeah but Mick…'

'Stop Jimbo, no buts – we need him, and yes I will have a word. Now pour me another Scotch and let's celebrate a successful job.' Billybob kept his mouth shut, it was obvious Conway wasn't going to listen to anything he had to say. All he knew was that he didn't like Ray Cole, not one little bit. And Conway didn't like Billybob. 'And you can fuck off as quick as you like.'

Chapter 14

Warren was starting to get seriously worried, there'd been no contact from Conway, or even Jimbo. He paced the carpet almost wearing a path through the already thin pile. Living room to the kitchen, then to the window, television on and television off. He was definitely showing signs of going 'stir crazy' forever sneaking a look through the net curtain.

In the weeks since he was first approached he'd let his hair grow, ok, not a quick job but it was considerably longer, combined with the fact he hadn't shaved for a few days and the stubble had thickened, he no longer quite resembled the face seen by millions on the television. Warren decided it was time for him to venture out into the big bad world. To prevent him from cracking up – a visit to the pub was in order.

The Sig? He could hardly take it with him and there was also the possibility that Conway might pay a visit while he was out. Warren went hunting through the kitchen drawers and found a screwdriver and a hammer, he thought about removing the panel below the bath, then thought again.

Too obvious.

Warren stood a while looking around the kitchen for a not-so-obvious place to conceal the Sig. Then he had it, and set about removing the plinth below the sink unit. Using the improvised tool kit, the plinth was removed without too much effort. Warren wrapped the Sig and holster in a kitchen towel and tucked it into the space. The plinth was wedged back into position – no screws. He had the notion that quick and easy access may be needed at some point. Standing in the centre of the kitchen he surveyed his handiwork, there was no obvious sign that anything had been tampered with. Pleased with the work, he returned the tools back to where he'd found them.

If he should visit one of the local pubs he was bound to draw attention to himself, something he was trying to avoid. On the other hand, the town centre would be busier, but this too he considered risky. Even though his appearance had changed over the past weeks, it was too soon to be walking the streets, there was still the chance an ex-colleague or copper on the beat would recognise him.

Decision made, it was to be one of the local pubs. *Ok*, he thought *I might rouse a bit of interest but it will last only for a couple of minutes until the next bloke walks through the door.*

The evening was drawing in, cooler now that the sun had disappeared. Warren breathed deeply as he left the stale smell of the tower block's lobby; the tang of the salty air blowing off the river was welcome. He stood a while taking it all in, the parking area was as normal. The only other people about were the same group of hoodies that had been there when he arrived and the Fiesta was still where it should be.

He pulled his own hoody over his head and walked out of the parking area without a second glance, not drawing any attention from the gang in the car park. This he thought was probably to Mick Conway's influence. Left along Great Thornton Street, onto Ice House Road, then onto Anlaby Road, he was heading for *The Eagle* on the corner of Coltman Street. It was easy to walk around the area without looking conspicuous or suspicious, the Hull Royal Infirmary was along the route, a route walked by many strangers to the area on their trek to visit friends and relatives. All the same he kept his head low, avoiding eye contact.

He took a deep breath as he opened the pub door and walked in, he was right, every head in the place tuned as he entered. Without making eye contact with the regulars he headed straight to the bar and gave the young girl behind the counter his best smile. He was surprised, it was his first time in the pub, it looked homely, like the old North London boozers.

'Pint of Foster's please love, and a whisky chaser,' he said, casually resting on the bar with his elbows.

She smiled and pulled his pint and then turned around to the optics for the whisky.

'Which whisky do you want?' She called over her shoulder.

'Bells will do nicely.'

Warren, watching her back, smiled at the way her short top rode up her body, exposing the flesh in the small of her back as she reached up to the optic.

'That will be five pounds twenty pence,' she said as she put the dram next to the pint.

Warren gave her a ten pound note.

'Get one for yourself,' he said.

'Thanks very much, I'll just have a half,' she cashed the ten pound note. 'You just visiting someone in the Infirmary?' she asked as she pushed his change across the bar.

'Bit nosey aren't you?' he said smiling.

Warren picked up his pint and sipped.

'I'm offended,' she said feigning hurt, 'not nosey – just interested,' she slid his change across the bar top.

'I've got some business in the city, staying up the road with a mate for a while.'

'Oh, do I know him?' she asked inquisitively.

'I wouldn't think so, not a bad pint this,' Warren replied changing the subject.

It didn't take long for the regulars to lose interest in him, the darts match taking place along with the football soon took care of the inquisitive.

Warren stood at the bar watching the football and making small talk with the barmaid. An hour and two pints later Warren decided to call it a night, a short but welcome respite from the flat.

'Well that's me, should be making a move.'

'Sure you don't want another?'

'Nah, better not, unless you're buying?'

'You're joking, on what they pay me in here,' they both laughed.

'Right I'm off, been nice talking to you,' Warren said as he zipped up his jacket.

'You never said what they call you?'

Definitely nosey, thought Warren.

'No I never did I. Be seeing you,' he said and stepped out onto Anlaby Road.

Standing outside the pub he looked around, he couldn't see anyone but he had that feeling, a feeling of eyes watching him. He shrugged it off *getting paranoid* he thought and started along Anlaby Road. The hairs on the back of his neck began to tingle, he was sure someone was following. He risked a look around as he crossed over the pedestrian crossing at Rawlings Way, he still couldn't see who was shadowing him, maybe Jimbo was under instructions to look out for him. Opposite the Hull Royal Infirmary, 'The Pharmacy' was shut down boarded up with steel shutters, it had definitely seen better days, looking tired and sorry for itself. By the side of the run-down building was a delivery alleyway leading around the back. Warren did a quick sidestep down the alley and waited. He could hear the quickening of footsteps, he was right, someone was following and whoever they were was starting to panic when they lost sight of him.

A figure appeared at the opening to the alleyway, Warren grabbed out with his right hand and pulled the figure into the gloom.

'I might have known it would be you,' he said as he pushed the skinny, denim clad body further down the passage. 'Conway sent you?'

'What do you think?'

'I fucking hate that,' said Warren.

'What?'

'There you go again, answering a question with a question.'

'No, Conway didn't send me. I can think for myself.'

'That right, so what are you expecting to get out of following me?'

Billybob was nervous, hopping from one foot to the other and back again, his hands in his jeans pockets. Warren was watching closely. Then Billybob took a step back produced a silver trimming knife from his pocket and extended the blade.

'What do you say to this then, now who's going to be laughing out of the other side of their face?'

Billybob laughed nervously as he passed the knife from one hand to the other with well-practised ease. Warren had no doubt in his mind the skinny youth had used it on more than one occasion.

'Been fitting some carpets?' said Warren as he suddenly reached out and grabbed Billybob's wrist. The knife fell to the floor as he bent the joint of the wrist and hand double and then there was a crack of bones as the wrist broke.

'Shit, fuck, fuck, you've bleedin' broke it.' Billybob screamed out like a girl.

'Got to be quicker than that Billybob.'

His would-be attacker fell to his knees, clutching his wrist with his good hand. Warren kicked out with his foot and the skinny bloke lost his balance and rolled over onto his back. Warren picked up the knife and put it in his own pocket.

'See Billybob, you just aren't good enough.'

He grabbed Billybob's right leg and dragged him around.

'What the fuck are you doing?' Billybob said between gritted teeth, the movement jarring his shattered wrist.

'Don't worry hillbilly, nearly done.'

Warren placed the foot on the concrete step that led into the rear of the shop creating a gap between the leg and the floor – then stamped as hard as he could on Billybob's knee.

Billybob almost howled with the pain as bone and tendons snapped. Immediately his jeans changed colour, darkening as blood flowed from the wound. Warren grimaced.

Billybob didn't notice – he was too busy crying.

Warren leaned over and clamped a hand over Billybob's mouth. The hillbilly tossed his head from side to side as he tried to yell his lungs out.

'Ssssh.' He smiled as Billybob writhed in agony on the floor. 'Someone might hear you. And that hillbilly is how a professional does it, no pissing about, in fast before the other bloke knows what's happening,' he said to the prostrate figure laying in the gloom of the alley. He took out his mobile and snapped a picture. 'At least the Infirmary is just across the road – if you can crawl that far.'

'Bastard... fucking... bastard,' Billybob sobbed out, in between breaths just before he passed out.

'I know. See you around hillbilly.'

Warren walked away. He thought his days of extreme violence were a thing of the past. *Funny how easy it comes back to you*, he thought. He took out his mobile and pressed speed dial one.

'Gemmell Strategies.' It was Bob.

'You're working late,' said Warren.

'Always available to take your calls Greg, no matter the time.'

'I'd appreciate it if you'd send an ambulance to...' Bob cut him short.

'Problem, you're not injured are you?' Bob asked, concerned.

'No, not me, I've just had a run-in with the numpty I told you about, Billybob the hillbilly, he needs medical attention ASAP.'

'I do hope this won't jeopardise the operation?'

'I shouldn't think so, anyway, send it to the old Pharmacy opposite the Hull Royal, at least they won't have far to go.'

'Anything further to report?'

'No, still waiting. I'll be in touch, sending a picture,' he hung up the call.

Back in the flat, Warren went through to the kitchen, took a glass tumbler out of the cupboard and poured himself a large measure of tequila, and downed it in one, swiftly followed by a *very* large tequila. He then went back through to the lounge, the bottle of firewater went with him, and feeling drained he dropped down onto the sofa.

Violence he thought was a thing of the past – so did the police counsellor, these days he would sooner try and talk himself out of a turbulent situation. He couldn't explain why he had done what he did, he knew it had been over the top when a slap or two would have done the job. He was wired and feeling remorse for his actions, he knew he wouldn't sleep and poured himself another, not before checking the Sig was still where it should be.

Chapter 15

As promised, Bob had alerted the emergency services. Ten minutes later the hillbilly was wheeled into the Accident and Emergency department of Hull Royal Infirmary. As in all cases of assault or suspected assault the police were notified.

'The damage is what you might expect if he'd been run-over by a ten ton truck,' the charge nurse told PC Brian Scott.

'The tone of your voice tells me you think otherwise,' Scott said.

'The evidence speaks for itself, the boot print on his leg was a big giveaway,' she replied sarcastically, 'and the finger marks around his wrist.'

'What happened to his wrist?' asked Scott.

'Someone snapped it in half.'

'Ouch!'

'Ouch is putting it very mildly, poor man must have been in agony.'

'Where is he now, can I have a word with him?'

'Sorry he's already in the operating theatre; trying to sort him out, with any chance they'll be able to save the knee and lower leg.'

'Did he say anything when he was brought in?' Scott asked as he scribbled in his notebook.

'He was delirious on the morphine the paramedics had given him, he kept saying, "tell Jim… Bo", or something like that.'

'Are these his personal belongings?'

Scott inclined his head towards a green plastic bag with the logo NHS.

'Yes, the clothes he was wearing and everything that what was in the pockets.'

PC Scott put on a pair of latex gloves and tipped the contents onto a vacant trolley. He began to look through the contents of the bag.

'Here we go,' he said as he found the wallet and opened it. Inside he found Billybob's driving licence. 'Oh this is good,' he said, 'this has really made my day.' The nurse looked on horrified at the comment. 'He's William Boland, AKA, Billybob. Wait 'til the lads back at the nick hear about this! It will probably be free teas all round in the canteen. He's well known to us, a right vicious little bastard – pardon my language. My reckoning is this Jim bloke he mentions is his cousin, James Boland – AKA, Jimbo, another one with a silly nickname. Think I'll give James a call and let him know what's happened.'

Chapter 16

Jimbo walked down the garden path to Conway's front door and rang the bell. Two minutes later the bolts were drawn and the door opened and Jimbo barged past.

'And good morning to you, just come marching in while I'm in the middle of my breakfast why don't you,' said Conway, still wearing his dressing gown, as Jimbo pushed passed him without wiping his muddy shoes, trampling mud along the highly polished solid oak flooring. 'Take your boots off before you go in there,' he shouted as he reached the lounge. Jimbo kicked off his trainer-boots and started pacing up and down the lounge carpet. 'What's got into you?' Conway demanded to know.

'Cole, that's who. What did I tell you Mick? You've got to rein him in, fuck him off,' Jimbo spluttered.

'What you going on about Jimbo?' Conway asked, quizzically.

'Billybob, Cole's only gone and put him in hospital hasn't he!'

'Calm yourself lad, sit your arse down.'

He ignored him and continued the pacing.

'He's wrecked Mick, fucking wrecked – crippled.'

Jimbo wasn't particularly over fond of his cousin, but he was family after all.

'Probably deserved all that he got, told him didn't I – leave off Cole. And will you STOP wearing a hole in my carpet? For fuck's sake sit down will you?'

Jimbo did as he was told and dropped down into one of the luxurious, soft leather chairs.

'Yeah but Mick, he did a proper job on Billybob, snapped his wrist in two and shattered his kneecap into fuck knows how many pieces. A gloating copper rang me last night, told me Billybob's leg was hanging in half when he was brought in – he's gonna be on crutches for months, if he's lucky. I could hear the copper sniggering at the other end of the phone, as he told me he might even lose the fucking thing.'

'So he'll have a wooden leg and walk with a limp, just means we'll have to find someone to replace him. I know he was your cousin but he's a little shit. Go and put the kettle on and make a brew.'

'Bet you wouldn't ask Cole to put the kettle on,' Jimbo mumbled to himself as he went through to the kitchen.

'What was that Jimbo?' Conway asked smiling to himself, knowing quite well what the scally had said.

'Nowt!' Jimbo called back.

'We'll have a coffee and then we're going to see your man.'

'Billybob?'

'Don't be fucking daft, what would I want to go and see him for?'

'I just thought…' He let it trail to a natural finish.

'Cole, you forgot I owe him some money?'

Jimbo tut tutted and shrugged his shoulders.

Warren woke on the sofa: he hadn't made it to the bedroom. 'Jesus,' he said out loud as he tried sitting up, only to collapse back in a heap. The result of too much tequila. He remembered why he didn't like the stuff. He eventually managed to heave himself off the sofa and make it as far as the bathroom where he threw up all he'd drank the night before into the toilet pan. More memories returned, he remembered what he'd done to Billybob and went back into the bathroom where he heaved again. He turned on the tap, filled the washbasin and plunged his head into the cold water, the shock made him gasp. Peering in the mirror through bloodshot eyes, his dark skin looked pale. He plunged his head again. With his face still dripping he went through to the bedroom and stripped off yesterday's clothes and collapsed onto the bed, his head spinning.

Once his head stopped doing somersaults, he eased himself off the bed, put on a pair of chinos and pulled a black T-shirt over his head. Then went through to the kitchen and started rummaging around in the drawers; he found what he was looking for – a pack of paracetamol. He popped two painkillers from the plastic blister pack and swallowed them dry. With a throbbing head he made himself a mug of strong instant coffee – black, in the lounge he sat and pondered. Warren even felt sorry for Billybob – a little, a twinge of guilt set in, he thought perhaps he should ring the infirmary to see how the hillbilly was.

He never made the call.

The mobile rang twice and then there was a hammering on the door.

'Come on Ray, open the bleedin' door,' Conway was out in the hall way banging on the steel plate.

Warren looked through the door viewer, Conway was alone. He unfastened the locks and slid the grating bolts free and opened the door.

'And to what do I owe the pleasure of this visit?'

'You smooth talking bastard,' he said and pushed passed. 'Hell pal, to say you look rough would be understating it, what the fuck was you drinking last night?' Warren stood aside to let the fat man past.

'Yeah well, just keep the volume down a little will you, I'm feeling a bit fragile,' he said as he shut the door and followed Conway into the living room.

'Heard you had a bit of a run-in with Billybob last night?' He dropped into the leather armchair.

'Only gave him what he was asking for,' Warren snapped back, defensively.

'Whoa, hang on matey, did I say anything different?'

'Sorry Mick, had too much of the Mexican stuff when I got back. The little shit must have been keeping tabs on me. I went down *The Eagle* for a pint and he was following me, so I collared him. When the little twat pulled a Stanley knife on me, well, that was the last straw, I just saw red.'

'I don't dispute that Ray, but according to Jimbo you made a right fucking mess of him. Did you have to go so heavy on him, he's only a kid?'

'Yeah one seriously fucked up kid. If it hadn't been me it would have been someone else, some poor fucker who couldn't defend themselves. Anyway, what can I do for you?'

'Thought I'd drop this over,' Conway took a roll of banknotes from his pocket and handed it over.

'Cheers,' Warren said as he opened the bundle and flicked through the notes. 'And what else has that lad of yours been telling you?'

'Nothing for you to worry about. I told him you must have had a good reason to show yourself at the meet.'

Warren smiled – it looked like he hadn't blown it after all.

'Where's the lad now?'

'When I told him I was coming to see you he decided he had to be somewhere. Not to worry, he's gonna turn up later.'

'Probably still smarting over the hillbilly.'

'Hillbilly!' Conway laughed, 'classic, fucking classic I'll remember that one.'

'You want a coffee, tea anything?

Warren walked through to the kitchen and turned on the kettle.

'No thanks, the other reason I came is to see if you fancy a bit more work?'

'Got to be better than sitting here on my arse all day,' Warren called out from the kitchen. 'What have you got in mind?'

'Remember a while back when I mentioned the cash van?'

Warren nodded. It was the thing he had be dreading. 'Yeah, you put something together?'

'As it happens I have, I take it you're still up for it?'

'Like I said at the time, if it's a workable plan, I'm in.'

'Good, it's tomorrow.'

'Bleedin' hell Mick, could have done with a bit more notice.'

'You haven't gone and booked a holiday to the Costas have you?'

'No, but all the same a bit more notice would have been good.'

'It's not a spur of the moment thing Ray, I got it sorted. I always like to work on short notice once I have the details ironed out, that way the team don't get time to blab about what's going down. So, this is how it's gonna work…' Conway spent the next half an hour going over his plan with Warren, surprisingly he was impressed, it looked like it could actually work as long as there was no interference from other sources.

Then there was another knock at the door, Warren reckoned on it being Jimbo. It was but he wasn't alone.

Warren went to the door and looked through the viewer.

'Who are this lot?' he asked nodding towards the door.

'Your team for tomorrow.'

Five dubious-looking individuals filed into the flat. Jimbo was last man in – he was carrying two plastic bags full of cans of lager. The team spread about the small sitting room and Jimbo distributed the booze. It appeared lager was the staple diet in certain quarters, along with chips.

'No thanks,' said Warren when offered a can.

'Please yourself,' Jimbo retorted and stood by the kitchen door.

'Hope you don't mind us using the flat for a little get-together, Ray?' Warren knew he had no say in the matter. 'Everybody got a drink? Ok, then I'll make the introductions, this is a good friend of mine you can call him Ray.'

Warren looked around the faces.

'Ray, what?' a suspicious, hard looking bald bloke wearing a leather bomber jacket asked.

'Doesn't matter, Russ,' Conway told him.

'Yeah, well, I like to know who I'm working with.'

'Leave it out Russ, he's a top bloke that's all that matters.'

Russ looked hard at Warren and tried to stare him out – Warren won that one.

'As you see, Russ is the gobby one. This bloke over here is Terry, most people just call him Tel.' Terry looked to be in his mid thirties, heavy set and tough as if he could be handy with his fists. 'Next up is Barry, he might look skinny but he's the best driver in the city.'

Barry and Warren exchanged nods.

Next in line was a short, grey haired, wiry bloke. 'This bloke here is Tony, bit of a wanker but he's good with the burning gear. That right Tone?'

'If you say so Mick.'

When Conway had finished making the introductions, Warren studied the faces in the room, trying to suss out who he was most likely to have bother with and came to the conclusion it would be the gobby Russ.

'Raymondo here has recently been involved with a hit similar to the one we are going to carry out. The difference being it was carried out by a highly skilled team from Ireland… not a team of wankers from Hull.'

'Fucking Paddies, I've shit 'em,' Russ interrupted.

'As I was saying, there is one other difference Ray was inside the van being hit, get my drift or do I have to draw you a picture? Obviously the hit was successful or Ray wouldn't be here with us now. And the bloke who organised the hit was Ray himself, so as he'll be running the operation he can tell you how this is going to work. And I don't want any shit.'

Warren stood up, straight and tall to emphasise his six foot two inches. There was a pronounced silence as all eyes turned on Warren. He stood and looked at each man in turn, holding their stares.

'Just in case you're wondering about me, I've known Mick for quite a while, but this is the first opportunity we've had to work together proper. Here's hoping it's profitable,' he said as he picked up a can of the coffee table.' Cheers,' he said holding his can high.

'Cheers,' they responded with the exception of Russ.

Mick laid a map of East Yorkshire on the living room floor and Warren took over the narrative as the small team looked and listened.

'Ok, as you know we're doing a hit on a Securicash armoured vehicle – you did know that didn't you?' Not everyone nodded, Russ just tried to stare Warren down. 'Just give me a minute will you,' he said to the group. 'Mick can I have a word,' he nodded towards the bedroom.

'He's pissing himself already,' he heard Russ say to the other.

'What's the problem?' Conway asked as he closed the door behind him.

'Don't think I can work with this Russ fella, can't see me getting any respect out of him.'

'That's ok, just sort him out,' Conway said casually, as if breaking someone's legs was something you did everyday as a matter of course.

'If I do we'll need a replacement.'

'Look Ray, if you think you need to earn some respect from the rest of the team just sort the fucker, he's a bit of a wanker anyway. Jimbo can always step in.'

'As long as you're ok with it?'

'Said so haven't I?' Conway was gradually losing his patience. 'Just bloody get it done with, I don't want to be here all bleedin' night.'

Warren knew he had to do something fast and serious, Russ looked as if he could be more than a match if he had a half a chance and Warren didn't intend to give him any chance at all. Both men walked back into Warren's lounge, Conway stood by the bedroom door. Russ was still sitting on the sofa, he looked to Tone who was sitting next to him and whispered something in his ear and then sniggered, it was obviously something derogatory aimed at Warren. Russ didn't try to hide the look of contempt that was showing on his face.

Before Russ knew what was happening, Warren reached down and grabbed him by the lapels of his jacket, pulled him to his feet and gave him an almighty 'Glasgow Kiss'. The attack took Russ completely by surprise, as the well-aimed head butt split his nose in two and spread mucus and blood across his face. Warren let go of the jacket and Russ fell to the floor, prostrate. Not wanting another 'hillbilly' coming after him with a trimming knife, Warren moved swiftly before Russ had a chance to recover. He grabbed the gobby man's arms, straightened them in front of him and stamped down as hard as he could with heel of his boot on each hand in turn. The finger bones crushed underfoot. It was all over in three minutes. The faces in the room sat in shock horror; no one said a word wondering if it was their turn next. Warren speculated what his counsellor back in London would have to say if he knew.

'Barry, Tel, go chuck the fucker out,' Conway ordered.

Blood and snot poured down Russ's face, his hands weren't in much better shape, the big hard-man actually had tears streaming from his eyes, not so much crying, but due to the fact his nose was spread across his face as Barry and Tone hoisted him up and dragged him out the door. 'Leave him in the car park,' Warren yelled after them.

'Drink up lads,' said Conway. 'That's the show over for tonight.'

It didn't take long for Barry and Tone to deposit Russ amongst the beer cans in the car park. 'Looks in a bad way,' Barry said to no one in particular as they came back into the lounge.

'Fuck him, let's get on with this.'

Warren laid out the plan – the hit was to take place on a quiet country road that cut through the common land of the Beverley Westwood. Barry would obviously be the getaway driver, Tone would ram the Securicash van with the skip truck and also use the burning gear. Jimbo was assigned the job of driving the lead vehicle and slowing down the van and Warren himself would be following behind. The job was to take place the next day.

'Any questions?' asked Warren.

'How do we know they will use the route across the Westwood?' asked Tel. The Beverley Westwood was a large expanse of grass and woodland that offered common grazing land rights for the hereditary pasture masters of the town

'It's not like when they are collecting from banks, they never deviate from routine according to Mick's contact.'

'How do we get inside the van, don't they have that paint that sprays you if the door is opened without the security code?' said Jimbo this time.

'That's where Tone comes in, he's got to hit the van so hard it goes over on its side and if the driver won't, or can't open up, Tone burns us a way in through the roof. The roof isn't as well armoured as the rest of the vehicle.'

'Any more questions?

'I've got one, will we be tooled up?' It was Tel.

'Just you and me. Mick tells me you can keep your cool. He's sorted us out with a couple of sawn-offs.'

'Right, any more?' No more questions. 'Ok that's it. Jimbo and Barry, I'll leave it up to you to sort the cars. Tone, Mick already has a refuse collection lorry sorted, here's where to pick it up.' Warren passed him a scrap of paper with an address written on it.

'That's a bin wagon to you Tone,' Conway said sarcastically, drawing a few laughs.

'I want you all back here at dinner time tomorrow and in the meantime keep off the booze. That's it, see you all tomorrow,' said Warren.

The small team drank up and drifted out of the flat.

'If Russ is still out there we'll drop him off at the infirmary,' Warren heard Tel say as they left.

The two men were now alone. 'Got a bit of a temper on you Ray.' Warren looked quizzical, he'd only done as he was told. 'I mean I know I told you to sort him, but fucking hell, the docs will have a hell of a job on trying to stitch his nose together.'

'He'll get over it – eventually. It did the job, the rest of the lads know where they stand. We'll get the job done a lot better without him.'

'Right then Ray, I'm away, I'll have someone drop the shooter off in the morning just before the off.'

Once he was alone again in the flat, Warren looked out of the window into the car park. He could see Russ being manhandled into one of the cars for the short trip to the Hull Royal Infirmary. Conway was coming out of the flat's foyer and heading for his Audi.

He sighed to himself, what a *fucking mess*, things seemed to be going from bad to worse, but he was the first to admit he had enjoyed taking out Russ, at least it vented some of his frustrations. In the bathroom he splashed his face with cold water then in the mirror he checked out his own forehead. Thankfully there was nothing more to show for the altercation than a small sore lump where it had made contact with Russ's nose, had he struck an inch higher he would have made contact with his forehead and probably caused damage to himself.

Chapter 17

After popping a couple of paracetamol for the headache that he knew would shortly follow, Warren made himself a coffee, and standing in the kitchen he picked up his mobile, pressed speed dial one and made the call.

Bob answered immediately.

'It's happening,' he said agitatedly into the handset.

'What's happening Greg?'

'The bloody armed robbery that's what. And on top of that I've only gone and put someone else in hospital.'

'Greg, calm down and take a breath, who exactly have you hospitalised?' Warren went on to give chapter and verse on why and how he had assaulted Russ Miller. 'Maybe we could turn that to our advantage.'

'In what way?'

'What's worse than a woman scorned? A disgruntled ex-colleague with a grudge, someone willing to inform the police of an impending crime, don't you think?'

'You're a devious bugger, I'll give you that. If it was ever to get back to Conway, Russ would be looking at more than a stay in hospital, he'd be a dead man walking.'

'Yes, the perfect scapegoat. We whisper in the appropriate ear and things will take their own course. Now tell me more about the robbery.' Warren went on to outline Conway's plan, time, route and the other members of the team. 'As we said, we cannot allow this to take place, more so now that firearms will be involved.'

'We will arrange for one or two of the participants in the operation to be picked up – two team members down and the operation won't be viable. During their interviews they will undoubtedly require the services of a solicitor; a solicitor who it would be reasonable to presume is retained by Mr Conway, and the seeds will be sown, there will be no doubt that Russ Miller is a confidential informant.'

'Think you can pull it off?'

'The time scale is tight, but all things being equal – yes I think we can, I'll organise a hospital visit by uniform when we're finished here.

'Just make sure Jimbo isn't arrested, I have a feeling I may need his help at some point.'

'That seems fair, I'll be in touch shortly.'

There were no two ways about it, Warren was relieved at the prospect of not having to take part. Now it was a waiting game to see what happened.

He didn't have to wait very long.

'Come on, open the fucking door.' Conway yelled as he hammered on the flat steel plate of the door. The door vibrated in its frame. 'Open up.'

'For fuck's sake Mick give me a chance to open the thing,' Warren yelled back as he slid bolts and unfastened locks.

'It's off, its fucking off,' he shouted as he barged past and headed straight for the booze in Warren's kitchen.

'What's off?' Warren asked keeping up the feigned shock.

Conway popped the tab on the can and came back with lager dripping down his chin. 'The fucking job, the heist, that's what's off. The coppers only went and picked up Tone and Tel.'

'Shit, what do you know?'

'Not much, I let them have access to my solicitor and he gave me the heads up, they've been picked up and held on trumped up charges. According to my brief "they are helping the Police with their enquires into historic crimes", whatever the fuck that means.'

'So, it doesn't mean they know about the job?'

'Oh for fuck's sake Ray, get real, why else would they have been nicked?

'So you're telling me we've been grassed up?'

'Looks that way to me, only one person would be doing that fucking Miller, fucking Russ Miller, the bloke you just sent to the Infirmary. I tell you what, he's dead, fucking dead.'

'You can't be sure it's him?'

'Oh I'm sure, I'm fucking sure no one else would dare to stitch me up. He's dead meat.'

'All that planning up the Swanny, not to mention I was looking forward to the pay day. Want me to sort him properly this time?'

'You sort him? No thanks that's something I'll enjoy doing myself.'

Conway ranted and raved for the next hour, making a dent in Warren's supply of lager. He was also feeling slightly pissed, matching Conway can for can. The difference being, Warren was drinking in celebration, in relief that the heist wouldn't be taking place.

As if he'd taken a magic potion Conway suddenly appeared sober.

'Anyway, onwards and upwards that's what I always say. We've got a busy week ahead of us.' For some reason he couldn't put his finger on, Warren was concerned. 'I've got a deal going with Big Jim Douglas and it's been brought forward. You interested?'

'What, after this last fiasco? I'm not sure that I need the agro mate.'

'Ray, what's done is done, we have to move on.'

'I'm not risking my bloody neck on a baccy run for Big Jim.'

'Come on Ray, would I waste your time on a piddling job, I've got monkeys for that stuff.'

Warren sat forward in his chair. 'Yeah, I've met them, remember?'

'Like I said, water under the bridge.'

'Plenty more Billybobs and the like in the sea?'

'Something like that.'

'Ok, start talking.' Warren was intrigued.

'Jim has – we have a shipment coming in from Holland in a few days, we've earmarked a location for the job and I'd like your opinion, what you reckon like, before we confirm.'

'Where?'

'Coming in by yacht, they're gonna bring it ashore at Blacktoft, a farmer who owns a stretch of river frontage owes us a favour.'

'More than a bit risky Mick, coming all the way down the river?' Warren gave him a concerned look.

'Not so, the *Seabird* is a regular visitor, they'll make radio contact with Customs as per usual and let them know they will be terminating the voyage at Goole. The goods will be long gone before they arrive and given a going over by the "rummagers".'

'Nice, you used this method before,' Warren asked.

'Not the same locations, but the same method. The knack is not to do it too often, you can get away with it two, maybe three times a year, any more and I think we'd be pushing our luck.'

'What are you bringing in – "brown stuff"?' he asked, referring to heroin.

Conway hesitated slightly before answering.

'Diamonds.'

'Bloody hell!'

'Done it before,' Conway replied, casually.

'What's the source, South African?'

South African "Blood Diamonds" was a very controversial subject; if he could get contact names of the original importers it would be more than just helpful it would be a major coup.

'Maybe, maybe not. To be honest I don't really care, a diamond is a diamond when all said and done.'

'If I agree I suss it out on my own, no Jimbo or bleedin' hillbillies, ok?'

'Sound fine to me.' Conway took an envelope out of his jacket pocket and passed it across to Warren. 'Thought you would say that. All the details are in here, once you're ok with it get rid of it, burn it, flush it, anything just get shut ok?'

Warren took the envelope and ripped it open.

'Will do,' he said as he scanned through the notes.

'Right then I'm off, I told the bloke who owns the land he might get a visitor sometime today, so no problems there, he won't come after you with a shotgun.'

Chapter 18

PC Brian Scott much preferred to be out on the streets, he wasn't very pleased to be sat watching the CCTV images taken from the traffic cameras along Anlaby Road. He sat back in his chair and rubbed his gritty eyes with his knuckles.

'Scotty how's it going?' Detective Inspector Bill Grimes asked, sticking his head into the video viewing room. 'You looking into the "pharmacy" mugging?'

'Not having much luck, yet sir,' he replied as the grainy black and white picture scrolled slowly on the screen.

'Have you heard anything from the hospital?'

'Called in myself to see if Boland was in any state to get a statement from.'

Scott pressed the pause button the DVD player, freezing the footage.

'Any good?'

'He was sat propped up in bed and wired up to goodness knows what. They fixed his wrist with metal work, but it's not looking so good for his leg, he's been told its touch and go whether it might have to come off, a case of wait and see. I almost felt sorry for him – almost.'

'Yeah well I don't have any sympathy for him, he's put plenty of others in the infirmary. Did you get anything out of him?'

'You've got to be joking sir, apparently he didn't see who attacked him, said he was bashed on the head, dragged down the alley and that's all he remembered. The next thing he knew the paramedics were putting him on a trolley and he passed out again.'

He turned to the screen again and pressed the play button.

'You believe him?' asked Grimes.

'Yeah, like I believe in fairies!'

'All I can say is he must have really pissed someone off for them to cripple him… hang on, spin it back a bit.' Scotty rewound the image, 'Right play it now – slowly.' The angle of the camera didn't offer the best of views; it was high on the traffic lights opposite the Hull Royal Infirmary primarily giving a view of the junction. 'Who do you reckon this might be?' In the periphery of the viewing area a figure very closely resembling Billybob appeared for a few seconds then jerkily disappeared from view.

'Boland?' Scott said as he rewound the image again and froze the screen.

'Could be.' Grimes leaned in for a closer look. 'Can you enhance the picture?'

'Sir, I'm a plod not a techie,' Scott said, turning to face the DI.

'Fair enough,' he smiled, he was all for a bit of banter. 'And who's this?'

A figure came out of the alley.

'Doesn't look like the same bloke who went down the alley, sir.'

They watched as a well-built figure wearing jeans and a hoodie came out of the alley.

'Bloody camera, can't make anything out. Looks like he could be talking on a mobile.'

'Calling for an ambulance?'

'Oh yeah Scotty, he cripples Boland then his conscience gets the better of him? Get real. But I tell you what, there's something about him, the way he walks. I swear I know him from somewhere. Get on to the town centre CCTV bods and see if he's picked up anywhere else.'

'Are you really that bothered sir, after all the little shit only got what he deserved?'

'Maybe he did, but I know that bloke from somewhere and I want to know where from. Let me know if you come up with anything.'

Chapter 19

Warren studied the timetable for the operation. The vessel, a Canadian designed *Vancouver 27,* a three berth yacht named the *Seabird,* was to head down the Humber at high-water, with the intention of reaching the meeting point sometime between 6 and 8pm the day after tomorrow. The farm had its own river frontage with a timber landing stage. The deal was to take place on board; the *Seabird* would be moored there for thirty minutes only, before carrying on its journey up the Ouse.

It seemed to be a straightforward operation, Warren had to hand it to Conway, he was a good organiser. There was even a sketch of the area marking the farmhouse and outbuildings. Warren went back through to the kitchen and made another coffee and then made the call.

'Gemmell Strategies.'

'Greg, how are things going?' John asked as he put the phone onto speaker mode.

'Fine, any fallout over last night's incident?'

'None as far as we are aware, just try not to make a habit of it. You have something to report?'

'Another name from the dossier has cropped up, Jim Douglas.'

'AKA: Big Jim, yes he's well known to all departments at home and on the near continent.'

'It appears Conway and Douglas are in cahoots on a big one.'

'How big?'

'Big enough. What do you know about diamonds?'

'Small pieces of hard glass, very expensive so I'm told,' John replied attempting to be humorous.

It didn't work.

'Yeah, funny – seriously, Blood Diamonds what can you tell me?'

'Well the abridged version goes something like this. A Blood Diamond, also known as a Conflict Diamond is a diamond mined usually in a war zone and sold to finance insurgency, pay for arms.'

'Is there a big demand?' asked Warren.

'There's always a demand for precious stones at the right price. The problem being these diamonds, or for that matter other precious stones mined in precarious areas have a detrimental effect on the worldwide market, therefore they are illegal as many come from areas of civil unrest and even civil war from places such as Angola and Sierra Leone,' Bob's voice said over the speaker.

'Well, it looks like we have a shipment coming in from Holland.'

'How soon?'

'In the next forty-eight hours, sailing right down the Humber to Blacktoft.'

'Strictly speaking Blacktoft is not on the Humber at all, it's on the north bank of the River Ouse where it joins the River Trent, then becomes the River Humber.'

'Whatever you say, John.'

Warren went on to give chapter and verse of how and when the operation was to take place and how 1.5 million Euros were to be transferred over the internet on completion of the deal.

'And your next move?' Bob asked.

'I'm going to go and give the location the once over, suss out any possible problems.'

'Keep in touch Greg, please give me a call on your return.'

'Will do.'

Warren hung up the call and checked his watch, lunchtime.

After lunching on a cheese and pickle sandwich washed down with a can of tepid cola, Warren readied himself for another trip down the A63. He debated whether he should take the Sig and decided against it, maybe next time – no definitely next time he told himself. After rummaging through the cupboards and wardrobe Warren found what he needed, a pair of wellington boots and a wax waterproof jacket and to complete the outfit a woolly pull-on hat. Warren changed his chinos for a pair of old denim jeans, put on the boots and jacket then checked himself out in the wardrobe mirror. *Ok, maybe I don't look like a real twitcher*, he thought to himself but it was the best he could do in the circumstances. But to the casual observer that's just what he would look like some boring birdwatcher.

The usual suspects occupied the parking area, the hoodies were there with their spliffs and cans and a couple of kids were having a kick about with a football. The Fiesta still occupied the spot where he'd left it two weeks ago; surprisingly it still had all its wheels. Warren thought this was probably down to Conway's influence.

He opened the driver's door and threw the rubber boots and jacket into the back then eased himself into the low seat. The Fiesta fired up first time, Warren fastened his seatbelt and drove out of the parking area. The A63 was a road he knew well, the main road leading west out of the city. The A63 changed to the M62 shortly after passing the Humber Bridge, Warren left the motorway at the village of Gilberdyke and then navigated the narrow country roads to Blacktoft.

The village of Blacktoft on the north bank of the River Humber, or as Warren had been corrected, the River Ouse, was deserted as he drove up in the Fiesta, more like a hamlet than a village. A few scattered properties stood back from the river frontage protected by a high grass bank. The public house however, *The Hope and Anchor* was perched high on the bank with splendid views across the river.

Warren drove the Fiesta into the pub car park. He manoeuvred the vehicle between a Range Rover and a VW Beetle, switched off and reached into the back for his jacket and boots. Dressed in the borrowed jacket and boots he walked up the high banking and admired the view. It was low water and the river ran in fast streams between the mud banks that were occupied by the feeding gulls. He fastened the jacket and pulled on the woollen hat and with his sketch of the area in his pocket he set off south down the foreshore looking for the timber jetty.

It was a tricky hike along the riverside, the supposed path became a sodden bog every few metres or so, with saltwater reeds growing to waist height hampering his progress. Ten minutes into the journey and Warren was stopped by a barbed wire fence. The security fence led off the land to the river's edge, there was no chance of going around without ending up waist deep in Humber mud. A plywood sign lay at angles with the fence, the words faded and weathered, *Private Property, Trespassers Will Be Prosecuted.*

'Yeah right, so much for ramblers having the right to ramble,' he said as he took of his jacket and laid it across the top wire strand. Carefully he put his weight on the jacket-covered wire and climbed over, then with a couple of good tugs retrieved his jacket – only now it had non-designer rips.

The terrain started to get rougher, with the reeds thickening and ground becoming even boggier and he found himself halfway up his wellingtons in muddy sludge. The field had little protection from the river at high water, even less protection from the easterly wind blowing down river. After a further five minutes tramping though the mire he eventually reach a small man-made inlet, its sides shored up with timber and a dilapidated wooden landing stage that straddled the inlet and slightly reached out into the river.

He'd found the spot.

The jetty was actually in better condition than he expected, made from 'Greenheart', a tough all weather timber used for structures that stood in water and were exposed to the elements all year round. Warren put one foot on the jetty, testing the safety of the boards – they creaked a little but seemed safe enough – and he stepped out over the mud below. He tucked his hands deep into his jacket pockets as the penetrating wind blew down the river. *I'm definitely a townie*, he thought to himself, as he hunched his shoulders and looked around. He looked up towards the sky, thinking that rain didn't seem very far away. It was a desolate place, there didn't look to be any occupied habitation for miles, although he knew the farmhouse couldn't be too far away.

Warren checked the sketch of the area looking for the location of the farmhouse, and set off inland along the edge of a ploughed field. The going was heavy, his boots stuck and the mud attempted to suck them off his feet with each step he took. He climbed a rickety stile, left the field and chose a route through a wooded copse, brushing away the branches as he went. The detached farmhouse stood 100 metres further on beyond the trees, a number of outbuildings looked to be derelict. Warren wondered what type of farm it was, no crops and no livestock, but then again if you were in cahoots with Mick Conway you were more than likely to be involved in something other than farming.

It looked as if the farmhouse was reached by a single lane track which led off a narrow road, Warren assumed the road led to the river at some point. He was happy, if happy was the correct word to use, the location was perfect for Conway and Douglas's needs, miles from anywhere.

'Bugger,' he said out loud when he realised he'd have to retrace his steps through the mud back to the car. Twenty minutes later, splattered with mud, he arrived at the *Hope and Anchor* and debated with himself whether to call in and have a pint and a bite to eat, but thought better of it. He put the muddy boots in the boot of the Fiesta, and was pleased to be back in the car as the rain came.

An old-fashioned real coal fire burned in the hearth of Mick Conway's living room. The heat from the fire was making Warren feel drowsy after his trip into the countryside.

'So, what do you reckon?' Conway asked as he passed over a cut glass tumbler of single malt.

'No tequila?' he asked, but pleased at the prospect of the malt.

'Fifteen years old this, it'll put hairs on your chest. Cheers!' He held the glass in a mock salute.

'As far as locations go, I've never seen such a dreary, isolated, uninhabited place in my life. Even the seagulls looked pissed off. It's perfect.'

'Hoped you'd say that.'

'Yeah, I had a good scout around and couldn't see any problems with the place as long as the transaction *is* carried out on board the yacht and quickly.'

'It will be, to be on the safe side the landowner has been told to make himself scarce for twenty-four hours,' he looked at his watch, 'from now. What I want to know is, are you in?'

'Thought you just wanted me to check it out?'

Warren sipped the malt, it was like nectar compared with the Mexican stuff.

'There's a lot riding on this one, I can't think of anyone better suited to the job.'

'Who else knows the details?'

'Me, Big Jim, you obviously and the Dutch.'

'What about the bloke who owns the jetty?'

'Na, just knows something's going on, he's happy as long as he gets his dosh.'

'Not even your lad Jimbo?'

The heat from the open fire was getting to Warren, he stood up and went to sit by the window.

'He's a good lad, but only gets told what he needs to know.'

'Ok I'm in, but let's keep it small scale, just me and the lad.'

'Sounds like a plan. Cheers,' he said raising the glass once more. 'Let's get some details sorted, first a top-up.'

Conway stood and walked over to the drinks cabinet and brought the malt back with him.

'You think Jimbo will hold it against me for what I did to his mate?' Asked Warren.

'He's not very happy about it, but he knows which side his bread is buttered.'

'And another question?'

'Ask away,' Conway replied as he topped up their glasses.

'If there's not going to be any problem with Customs and Excise why the hell is the deal being done in the back of beyond?'

'A good question which deserves an answer.'

Conway smiled and with his index finger he gave a 'knowing' tap to the side of his nose.

'Well?'

'I have a little transaction of my own going down on the side. They're bringing in a package for me.'

'For Christ's sake Mick, you don't do things by halves do you?'

'In for a penny in for a pound, that's what I always say. All you have to do is check the package and hand over the readies.'

'And the sparklies, how do I know if they're real and I'm not coming away with a pile of broken glass?'

'They've already been authenticated in Amsterdam. You know the boxes that the security people use? Where a dye explodes if the box is tampered with, or opened without the proper code? Well they're in one of them. The only people who know the code are me, Big Jim and our contact in Amsterdam. I tell you what the code is and you make sure the rocks are in the box. If you are happy with things, you put the authorisation code into the laptop and transfer the dosh!'

'And your package?'

'That's an easy one, again you check the package is what it's supposed to be and then pay the man, simple. What can go wrong?'

About a thousand and one things, thought Warren.

'Names?' he asked.

'No names, one guy is Dutch and the other is English, if anybody he's the one to watch. Know what I mean?'

'Well I guess I'd better leave you to it.' Warren said as he stood up and walked into the hallway. 'You'll tell Jimbo what's what?' he asked as he put on his jacket and boots.

'I'll tell him to give you a bell and you can sort out the details between you, ok?'

'As you said Mick, sounds like a plan,' Warren replied as he walked down the garden path towards the Fiesta.

Warren headed back to the flat on Great Thornton Street and made his scheduled call to Gemmell Strategies.

'It's on for tomorrow, will you be taking any action?'

'Very short notice Greg, I can't confirm either way at this stage but probably not.'

The coffee machine gurgled and hissed its dubious contents into the glass jug. Bob walked across the office to the hissing machine, took two fresh cups from the tray and poured the contents of the jug.

'Well John, what do you think?' he asked as he returned, putting the cups down on the desk.

'I think we should leave well alone,' he replied as he picked up his coffee. 'We shouldn't be too hasty.'

'That's what I thought – at first, too soon, but I can't see a more lucrative opportunity like this arising any time in the future.'

'So what are you saying?'

'You *know* what I'm saying – we intervene.'

John sat forward in his chair, elbows resting on the desk making a temple with his fingers.

'Extremely short notice to launch and organise a detailed operation.'

'Agreed, as there is no time for elaborate planning, we need someone who can think on their feet.'

'And whoever we choose would have to be expendable should anything untoward happen. Warren's nobody's fool.'

'Have you anybody in mind?'

'As it happens we do have someone who fits the bill, Peter Stapler.

Stapler had worked for the organisation for the past two years, and had been a very useful asset. Of late he was becoming somewhat of a liability, far more inquisitive than his pay grade and was also nearing the end of his tenure with the department.

'Where is he now?' asked John.

'The French "deal" is now complete and by all accounts he should be back in the country.'

Bob picked up the phone and dialled.

Chapter 20

Warren with Jimbo in tow followed the same route he had taken the previous day from the *Hope and Anchor* to the rendezvous point. Rain was falling steadily, making the going even harder, Warren was pleased he was wearing the borrowed wax jacket and rubber boots.

'Fucking hell Ray, if you'd told me what we was up too I'd have worn a pair of wellies,' Jimbo said as he tried to kick the clinging mud from his trainers.

'You obviously weren't a boy scout Jimbo,' he laughed. 'What's the motto? Be prepared! That's it.'

'Shit,' said Jimbo, as he once again got stuck in the mud.

As they approached, over the reeds growing on the creek bank, the tall single mast of the *Seabird* came into view. She was exactly where she was supposed to be. A further 100 metres on Warren called a stop.

'Well there she is.'

'Can't see anybody, you would have thought one of them would be keeping an eye out for us,' Jimbo said, pensively.

'Mmm,' Warren thought the same. 'Right matey, this is what we're going to do. This time you're the watcher, find yourself a good spot and you keep a good eye on the boat and the area.'

'Watcher, for fuck's sake Ray, we don't need a watcher.'

'Jimbo, you said it yourself, you thought there should be someone on lookout. There's a lot more at stake on this job than a piddling packet of "H", know what I mean? If there's trouble I want you to get the fuck out of it, understand? I don't want you taking any chances.'

'Yeah but…'

'No yeah buts, pal. If you see anything call me on the mobile, I'll have it on vibrate. On the other hand, should you think anything's happened to me, don't come charging in like the cavalry, just get the fuck out of it, ok?

Jimbo wandered off to the left, looking for a good vantage point amongst the tall reeds. 'Shit,' Warren heard as Jimbo splashed about in the salt marsh. He smiled to himself and carried on. There was no need for a stealthy approach, Jimbo was making enough noise for the two of them and, after all, he was expected.

The nearer Warren got to the *Seabird*, the more his police instinct kicked in, something just didn't seem kosher. Jimbo was right, why wasn't anybody on deck? Now was the time to adopt a different mindset, he backed away and circled around and approached the yacht from the aft, with the river front behind him. It was quiet, too quiet. The breeze rustled through the reeds, he could hear the waves lapping against the *Seabirds* hull, the only other sound was the screeching of the seagulls gliding on the wind. Slowly and hesitantly, he approached the Greenheart timber jetty. The wood was slick and wet from the high tide spray, the Seabird was moored to the timber structure.

The spray from the river covered his wax jacket like a fine mist, he contemplated calling out to anyone below decks, changed his mind and reached inside his jacket and released the safety clip on his Sig holster for quick access. Holding onto the bulwark of the Seabird, he placed one leg on board and waited, nothing, now with his full weight on the deck he could feel the *Seabird* shift against the jetty. Slowly he made his way aft and stopped at the cockpit and listened: silence. His right hand reached into his jacket and rested on the butt of the Sig. Warren placed his hand on the handle of the sliding door leading into the accommodation area, slowly he slid the door aside and stepped down into the galley.

The two crew members were knelt on the floor with their backs towards him, bound at the ankles and their hand behind their backs fastened together with plasti-cuffs. Parcel tape wrapped around their mouths and heads. 'Shit,' said Warren as he took another step into the cabin.

He didn't realise it but he'd stepped into hell.

'Far enough, Cole, don't turn around, keep your eyes to the front.' He didn't see who the voice belonged to. Warren stopped dead, he hadn't heard the silent approach, never mind have time to pull out the Sig. 'Easy now, take your hand out of your jacket, slowly and keep looking in front.'

He removed his hand from inside the wax jacket and let both arms hang by his side. Before he had time to speak or turn around Warren felt a hand grab his neck, a well-practised grip grabbed his neck and found the carotid artery, pressure was applied, suddenly he felt light headed and fell to the floor as the circulation to his brain was cut off. The two men turned to see Warren fall to the deck unconscious.

His assailant removed the Sig from its holster, and placed it on the galley table. Next he went through Warren's jacket pockets and found the envelope containing the twelve thousand pound drugs payment. The unexpected guest pocketed the cash; he was already in possession of the diamonds and heroin. He turned and with a gloved hand picked up the Sig and released the safety catch. Kneeling close to Warren's body, he took a hold of his right hand and held the fingers around the pistol grip and trigger. He struggled with Warren's weight as he manoeuvred him into position, once he was balanced he pointed the Sig at the back of Dutchman's head and execution style he pulled the trigger. His partner in crime, distraught, tried to twist and turn but no amount of effort was going to save him, BANG, he fell forward onto the deck as the bullet entered the back of his head and exploded through the front splattering brain and bone around the small cabin. As well as Warrens fingerprints on the fired weapon, his clothes were covered with GSR, gun shot residue.

Calmly and quickly he double checked he had left no evidence, it wouldn't be long before Warren regained consciousness. He was happy, he left the *Seabird* closing the cockpit hatch behind him. He had never been there.

Three minutes later Warren slowly stirred, from the prone position he managed to get to his knees, his head felt as if he'd been asleep for a week. He tried to shake the fuzziness away. He lifted his hands to his face, that was when he realised the Sig was in his hand. Warren was confused, until he saw what was left of the small crew and the reality hit him, his weapon had been used for the execution.

'Ahh, shit,' he said out loud when he realised he had been well and truly stitched up.

The money was gone from his pocket. 'That's all I bloody need,' he said. There was no doubt in his mind that the diamonds would also be missing. Still on his knees he crawled over to the two bound men, a quick glance told me it was pointless in checking for a pulse, they both had gaping holes in the front of their skulls where the bullets exited.

Warren felt sick. He managed to reach the small galley basin before retching, he ran the faucet and splashed cold water over his face, then he remembered Jimbo was on lookout. Why the hell hadn't he seen the gunman? But then again he'd told Jimbo to get out fast if trouble started.

On wobbly legs Warren he made it to fresh air of the deck. He pulled himself together and climbed over the side of the *Seabird* onto the wet timber planks of the jetty. Retracing his route through the mire he headed off to where he had left his watcher. No sign of Jimbo, then he saw a trace of blue denim. Jimbo was amongst the reeds – he lay face down in the mud, barely visible amongst the vegetation. Warren dropped down to his knees and put his fingers to the young man's neck, there was a pulse.

'Thank God,' he said out loud as he turned the younger man onto his back. 'Jimbo, can you hear me?' he gently shook him by the shoulders. 'Come on wake up, we've got to get out of here!' Jimbo's eyes flickered and opened. 'Good lad.'

'What's happened?' he asked as he tried to sit up.

'We got turned over, that's what happened.'

Jimbo ran his hand across the back of his head, his fingers came away bloody.

'Fuck,' he said as saw the blood. 'The money – the diamonds?'

'Gone mate, fucking gone!' Warren offered a hand and pulled him to his feet.

'What about the couriers?' he asked as he rocked on his feet.

'Not as lucky as us, had their brains blown out – with MY Sig!'

'You didn't did you?' Panic set in Jimbo's face.

Warren ignored the comment.

'Looks like a professional hit, someone took me out as soon as I went below deck on the *Seabird*.'

'You telling me the truth, Ray?'

'Oh yeah, I topped them and left a live witness, you. 'Course I'm telling the truth. Whoever it was wasted them execution style, on their knees with a bullet through the back of the head, bullets from my gun and my prints all over them.'

'Don't wanna be in your shoes when you tell Mick. My bleedin' head hurts.'

'Yeah well, that is going to be a bit of a problem.'

'A bit of a problem is an understatement, pal,' Jimbo said. 'I reckon you're fucking dead mate, a dead man walking.'

'Oh you're such a cheerful bugger. One question Jimbo, did you know what was going down today?'

'No idea until you told me an hour ago.'

'This was all secret squirrel stuff, know what I mean? Nobody other than Big Jim, Mick and the fellas on the boat knew.'

'What about the Dutch contact?'

'Na, he stood to make a lot of cash. Why steal your own diamonds? Don't make sense.'

'None of it makes sense.'

'Come on let's get out of here. Bit of a trek back, you manage ok?'

'Ray, can the bullets from the Sig be traced back to you?'

'Now there's a question.' Jimbo turned around and started to make his way back to the *Seabird*. 'Now where do you think you're going?'

'To torch the fucking thing, they won't find any bullets at the bottom of the river – maybe a few burnt bones but no fucking bullets.' Warren smiled as he followed the younger man, who was caked in mud from his trainers to his neck. He liked the notion that Jimbo did have his back after all. 'But I can't help you with the bigger problem.'

'Bigger problem, is there one?'

'Mick, you going to give him a call?'

'Some things are better said face to face, Jimbo.'

'You're a brave man Ray, a fucking brave man.'

Back on the M62, heading into the city, black smoke from the *Seabird's* exploded diesel tank could be seen for miles. Warren was glad to be back in the relative safety of the Fiesta as the first of the emergency vehicles passed them going in the opposite direction. Little conversation took place during the drive back to the city. Jimbo sat quiet, holding a dirty handkerchief to the cut on the back of his head.

'You want dropping off at the Infirmary?' asked Warren.

'Nah, I'll be ok, had worse.'

End of conversation.

The drive gave Warren time to think. Conway, Douglas and the contact in Holland were the only people who knew what was going down and when. It was a win-win situation for all involved, yet someone had had the bottle to sell them out and take the spoils for himself, again he asked himself the same question, who would have the balls?

Warren wasn't looking forward to telling Conway there was no longer any drugs, money or diamonds. His mobile rang, he checked the number and it was Conway, Warren disconnected the call. Three miles down the road the mobile rang once more, it was Conway. This time Warren turned off the mobile. Conway could wait, more thinking time was needed.

Warren pulled the Fiesta up outside of Jimbo's home. 'Make sure you give that wound a good wash, and put some antiseptic on it,' he said to Jimbo as he was easing himself out of the car.

'Yes, Mother,' Jimbo replied, sarcastically.

'Give you a call later – see how you are?'

'Whatever.'

Chapter 21

Warren dropped Jimbo off and then headed for the sanctuary of the 'safe' flat on Beverley Road. He was in need of some alone time, time to think without the fear of Conway bursting through the door at any time demanding to know what went wrong. He knew he would have to face him at some point soon, but not yet. He parked the Fiesta around the back of the hairdressers, climbed the metal staircase and punched in the combination lock number. Once in the flat he stripped off his muddy clothes, threw them into the washing machine and set it going. Wearing just his boxes and socks he went through to the kitchen and found the tequila bottle

The smell of chemicals from the hairdressers below invaded the place, Warren opened the window hoping the fresh air would take away the fumes. He sat in front of the gas fire. 'Beggars can't be choosers,' he said out loud as he poured himself a measure. Sitting on the sofa in his underwear with the tequila in hand, he tried to piece things together. He just couldn't fathom it, why was he set up to take the fall?

In the meantime he had a call to make using speed dial one.

'Unfortunately we are unable to take your call, please call back during office hours.'

'You are joking me?' He yelled down the phone. 'You're supposed to be available twenty-four seven!'

'Thank you for your call.' End of – no option for leaving a message.

Warren couldn't comprehend what he'd just heard. *Answer phone?* He dialled again – the same message. He thought perhaps there was some legitimate reason no one answered and dropped the phone beside him on the settee, thinking he'd give it fifteen minutes and try again.

The mobile began to ring. 'Thank you Lord,' he said as he picked it up expecting the call would be from Bill or John. He glanced down at the screen it wasn't who he was expecting, it was Conway again – he cancelled the call. Picked up the television remote and switched on the television just in time for the local news.

'The emergency services were called out to a fire on a boat moored at a private wharf near Blacktoft, in East Yorkshire. The Fire and Rescue Service managed to put out the fire, it is believed there were two fatal casualties. It has not been determined if the fire started accidentally at this stage. Further enquiries into the incident are ongoing.'

'Oh for fuck's sake,' said Warren, 'the bloody thing was supposed to sink!'

There was no doubt in his mind that he was in serious trouble, in the shit right up to his neck. The *Seabird* was still afloat, no matter about in what condition, it meant the bodies of the couriers could eventually be identified along with the bullets that had killed them – with Warren's fingerprints and DNA on the casings.

Chapter 22

Warren couldn't put it off any longer, he knew Jimbo would be telling Conway about the 'cock-up' as soon as he had the opportunity. Once his clothes had come out of the drier he dressed and decided time was up, he had to bite the bullet and face Conway.

He pulled up the Fiesta outside Conway's home, taking a couple of deep breaths to compose himself. He climbed out of the car and clicked the lock. Confidently, he walked down the path and pressed the front door bell. The door opened.

'So you decided to show yourself! Why have you been ignoring my fucking calls?' Conway demanded to know as Warren pushed passed and went straight to Conway's drinks cabinet. 'Well fucking answer!'

'So, the lad told you what happened?' Warren said as he took of a bottle of tequila out of Conway's drink cabinet.

'Course he fucking did, like you should have done two fucking hours ago!'

'Tell you what, it looks to me like you set me up, there were no fucking diamonds or drugs. You wanted me to take the fall for whatever it is I don't know about,' Warren bluffed.

'What? You fucking crazy?'

'From where I'm standing Mick, looks like you used me and the lad as patsies.'

'Get fucking real! Just tell me where my bleedin' diamonds and cash are!'

'You should know, you set the deal up, and me up while you were at it.' He poured a generous measure into a cut glass tumbler.

'Like fuck I did.' Conway snatched the bottle and poured himself one, grimacing as he swallowed the Mexican firewater. 'Hate this stuff. And what the fuck do you mean – I should know?'

'Stands to reason, very few people knew what was happening, and I know it wasn't me. How do I know this wasn't your idea all along? Bump off the couriers, steal the drugs and the rocks? Looks like a nice little low risk earner to me.'

'Why would I do that? I'd have just got you to do it in the first place,' Conway spat out.

'Keep it looking kosher to your investors? Make a mug of me, get whoever it was to give Jimbo a tap on the head, use my gun to execute the couriers and it all points my way. Nice one.'

Conway calmed. 'Look Ray, I can assure you I know fuck all about it. I had a lot of money invested in this fiasco. On the other hand if I find out you've ripped me off, you're dead. Get me?'

'So what happens now?' asked Warren.

'What happens? What happens now my friend…'

'So we're still friends?'

'A figure of speech. As I was saying, you find whoever it was ripped me off and deal with them.'

'Any ideas who could be behind it?'

'You said it yourself, no fucker knew. So no, I don't have an effing clue.'

'Thought you'd say that, any chance of some cash to tide me over?' Warren asked keeping up the pretence.

'Piss off – go rob a bank!'

Chapter 23

The tarmac looked slick in the floodlights as the rain steadily fell, puddles formed on the tarmac of the Humber Bridge viewing area car park. A solitary vehicle, a black BMW with tinted windows stood beneath the floodlights. Condensation started to build up on the windows as John and Bob waited.

In the rear view mirror, John saw a vehicle approaching. 'I think he may be here.' A dark coloured Range Rover pulled up beside them, the driver killed the ignition and turned off the lights. He reached over into the back seat and picked up a briefcase. A moment later Peter Staples climbed out of the Range Rover, shut the door behind him and opened the rear door of the BMW and lowered himself in.

'Evening,' he said, wiping the rain from his face.

'You're late,' John said, sternly.

'Better late than never,' not even trying to justify being ten minutes late.

'So, your report?' He left the question hanging.

'No problems,' he passed over the briefcase into the front.

Bob put the case across his knees and opened the latches. 'No, it went easier than I expected. But you never told me there would be two of them.'

'Two? We didn't know ourselves. We were led to believe Cole would be operating on his own.'

'He had a young guy with him, but as I said, no problems – contract fulfilled.'

'The crew of the yacht?'

'As I've said, the contract had been completed.'

'Good,' he passed over a bundle of cash. 'This is what we agreed.' Staples didn't check, just put the money in his coat pocket.

'We have a freelance operation we'd like you to take care of,' said Bob as he turned to face Staples. 'Totally off the books of course, should anything go wrong we will be denying all knowledge. Interested?

'Usual fee?'

'Plus a substantial bonus once the task has been completed.' Staples raised his eyebrows, he was already being well paid.

John opened the glove compartment and gave Staples two further envelopes. 'Your retainer and the details of the contract. A speedy conclusion would be appreciated.'

Staples never spoke. He nodded and returned to the Range Rover. Once inside out of the rain he opened the larger of the two envelopes.

His target was Raymond Cole.

'So,' said John hesitating slightly, 'I think we should inform our uniformed colleagues that Greg, alias Raymond Cole is wanted in matters relating to terrorism. And he is to be apprehended as a matter of urgency and to be held in isolation without questioning and then handed over to us.'

'Should Staples not fulfil the contract first I take it?'

'Exactly.'

Chapter 24

Back in the Great Thornton Street flat, the central heating had kicked in. Strangely, Warren felt at home. He was wired from the day's events and his run-in with Conway, which had gone better than he anticipated, and settled for a mug of strong instant coffee. He walked over to the window and looked down into the parking area, no change, the same depressing view and the same group of lads with their tinnies.

Three more times he tried to contact Gemmell Strategies and again received the same voice mail message.

This just isn't right, dropping the mobile onto the coffee table and sitting back on the settee he picked up the coffee. His mind was working overtime – going into possibilities he didn't want to believe but there seemed to be no other alternative, on the face of it Bob and John were responsible for recent events. The more he thought about the answer phone the more certain he was. For the last time he picked up the mobile, if Bob and John had gone incommunicado *was* he still being monitored? *Yes*, he thought *well this works both ways*. He took the back off the mobile and removed the battery. 'And fuck you too,' he said as he put the unassembled mobile down on the table.

Warren picked up his mug and swallowed the now cold coffee, put on his jacket and boots and picked up the car keys. Taking the stairs he went down to the parking area, nodded to the group of lager swilling lads and popped the bonnet of the Fiesta. 'Now where is it?' He said out loud as he searched for the tell-tale blue light of the tracking device the Fiesta had been fitted with. He saw the flashing light reflecting underneath the steel battery tray. He reached in with his right hand. 'Got you – you bugger.' Twisting his arm at the wrist he managed to get a firm grip of the silver metal box no larger than a box of matches and tugged, the device came free trailing the feed wires, which he separated and tied off to prevent a short circuit. The blue was still flashing, indicating it also had an integral battery.

He dropped it to the concrete and stamped down hard with his booted foot, the light stopped, picking up the pieces he put them in his jacket pocket and walked towards Anlaby Road. At the traffic lights at the corner of Ice House Road he crossed Anlaby Road and walked up the Park Street Bridge, the road bridge over the main arterial railway track into Hull's Paragon Station. At the other side of the bridge was a Tesco superstore. Specification or style wasn't a necessity for his need; he bought two of the cheapest unlocked pay-as-you-go mobile phones he could, Nokia 106s. One for contacting Conway, the other for private calls as needed, along with half a dozen SIM cards.

Back in the flat, he did some more thinking while he reassembled the 'spook' mobile and transferred the contact list to one of the new phones. Events had moved on much quicker and he was deeper in than he ever expected. He needed a friend other than Jimbo, one who knew what they were actually doing; there was only one name that came to mind, Detective Inspector Bill Grimes. With the cheap pay-as-you-go Nokia mobile in his hand he decided he had no other option and tapped in a text message. "Need to meet, urgent, Warren." He punched in Grimes's number and waited – impatiently.

It wasn't long before a reply came back and a flurry of messages followed. The meet was arranged for the same evening at *The Black Boy* in the old town, chosen for its out of the way location. Warren walked through the back streets to *The Black Boy,* feeling conspicuous, drawing little comfort from the Sig tucked away inside his jacket. He would have sooner left it behind, but felt the need of the extra security it offered regardless of the risk.

It was only a ten-minute walk to the pub through the back streets, he judged the journey to arrive with time to spare, time to check the place out. Even though he must have visited the pub dozens of times since he first came to the city he still wanted to give the exits a once over. Once he was satisfied everything was ok he ordered at the bar. With a pint of lager and a whisky chaser he chose a table away from the pub doorway, but one that still afforded a good view of the exits. He trusted Grimes – but would he come alone? Warren kept asking himself. He knew if the boot was on the other foot he'd be tempted to bring backup.

The clock ticked its way around – eight o'clock, he had been waiting for the past fifteen minutes. Grimes said he'd be there by quarter to. Then a text came through on his mobile, it was Grimes. "Been held up at work, be with you in five."

DI Bill Grimes, still dressed in his formal work clothes; a pinstriped two-piece suit, arrived five minutes later and walked straight to the bar. Casually looking around, saw Warren and gave a slight incline of the head. 'Stella, please mate,' he said to the barman.

Warren left his drink on the table and walked over to join Grimes. 'I'll get that,' he said to the young bloke behind the bar passing over a five pound note, 'and I'll have a single malt.'

'I'll need more than that,' he said pointing to the fiver.

He took the five back and handed over a tenner. 'And one for yourself.'

'Cheers, I'll take a half,' he passed Warren back his change.

'Shall we?' Warren nodded towards the rear table.

'Tell you what Greg, could have knocked me over with a feather when I got your text, totally unexpected. Thought I'd seen the last of you,' said Grimes as he sat down and took off his tie and stuffed it in his jacket pocket. 'So, what's all this about?' He picked up his Stella and sipped

'I'm well and truly in the shit, Bill.'

'I'm listening.'

'You in a hurry?'

Grimes could tell from Warren's appearance something was amiss, no smart suit or shiny shoes and the hair, no longer a close crop cut, but longer – no style, like the beard.

'Not at all mate, I'm here as long as you need me – well, until we get pissed or they throw us out,' he said trying to lighten the atmosphere.'

'You remember that day I was called into the Super's office?'

'Yeah I remember, you walked out with those two blokes never to be seen again – until now that is.'

'Well I'm telling you, I wish I'd never fucking met them.' He hesitated, picked up the malt and knocked it back in one. 'It goes something like this…'

For the next hour and two pints, Warren gave Grimes chapter and verse of what had happened from his meeting with the Suits: the assumed identity, the firearms training, the drug deal and how he had been set up on the *Seabird*.

'Bloody hell Greg, that's some story, straight out of some paperback crime novel. No wonder you're bloody paranoid.'

'What brought you to that conclusion?'

'You've never kept your eyes still since I arrived, constantly checking the place out.' Grimes signalled to the barman for another round of drinks. 'That's it, you've told me everything?'

'Not quite everything, the gun that was used to execute the crew of the *Seabird* – it was mine.'

'So, when they dig the bullets out at the post-mortem they can link them to you?'

'Only if, and it's a big if, Bob and John themselves have linked me to the weapon.'

'Where's the gun now?' Warren gently tapped the side of his jacket. 'For fuck's sake Greg, you shouldn't be carrying that through the streets. You've got to let me hand it in.'

'Sorry Bill, I can't do that, if I do I may as well admit it was me who shot those two blokes. The evidence is stacked up against me.'

Silence.

'I take it from what you've told me you were responsible for putting William Boland in hospital?'

Warren smirked. 'Didn't know that was his name, he was a little shit. I called him Hillbilly. It was one of those situations, know what I mean? Impulse, if I'd just slapped his wrist, the next time he fancied having a go I wouldn't have seen him coming.'

'I had one of the uniform lads trail through the CCTV near where he was found, all we could see was a grainy back view of someone walking away from the alley. I said to Scotty, the bloke looked familiar, the way he walked, held himself. Never in a million years thought it would be you.'

'A kid with attitude. Had to be done.' He picked up his pint, seemingly studying the condensation running down the glass. 'You going to help me?'

'I'll think about it while I go for a piss.'

Grimes stood and went to the gents. Warren sat waiting impatiently for his return, tearing a beer mat into tiny pieces while checked out the faces.

The DI returned and sat down. 'Ok.'

'Thought you were going to say no, want another?'

'No thanks, had enough.'

'So what is it you want me to do?'

'Raymond Cole, according to my "handlers" he's on remand in Belmarsh, can you get me anything on his current situation?'

'That it?'

'Gemmell Strategies, who they are and which department they're linked to, anything you can get me.'

'In the meantime what are you going to do?'

'That raises another problem. They're supposed to be available twenty-four seven, seems they've gone off the radar. I haven't been able to contact them for twenty-four hours. I'm going to take a drive out that way when we're finished here.'

'Is that wise?' asked Grimes. Warren gave him a quizzical look. '*Because* you're half pissed?'

'You do have a point. Maybe in the morning.'

'Right then, I'm heading off,' Grimes stood and eased the crick in his back. 'I'll be in touch.' He held out his hand. 'Text me that phone number.'

'Keep it to yourself?' Warren asked looking into his eyes, keeping a firm grip of Grimes's hand.

'No problem, pal.'

The next morning before paying a visit to Gemmell Strategies, Warren packed his meagre belongings into his rucksack. It was time to move on – *but to where?* he asked himself. If he stayed put, his so called handlers would soon have him under surveillance and on top of that Conway or one of his cronies could pay a visit at anytime, day or night and it wasn't a risk he fancied taking.

The flat on Beverley Road was also an option he ruled out and at one point considered moving back into his own home, but decided against it for the time being. A bed and breakfast seemed to be the logical answer. Twenty minutes after locking the Great Thornton Street flat he was pulling into the car park of a budget hotel along Springbank, *The Shangri La*. Warren chose the hotel for its close proximity to the town and the fact that the parking area was around the back, out of casual view.

He backed the Fiesta into a space, facing the car park entrance should he have need to leave in a hurry. With his rucksack slung over his shoulder he walked around the front of the hotel, up six concrete steps and into the dated foyer. A young female receptionist sat behind the desk – busy.

'Excuse me? Warren said to the girl behind the desk filing her fingernails. 'You have a vacancy?'

'Thirty-five pounds a night and that doesn't include breakfast,' the girl behind the reception desk said without even looking up.

'Sounds ok to me,' he said, dropping the rucksack to the floor.

'How long are you staying?' She asked, putting down the nail file.

'Probably a week or so.' Warren replied as he looked around at the shabby foyer, hoping it wouldn't be for too long.

'Fill this in,' she said passing over a registration form, 'and I'll need your credit card details.'

'Cash ok?' He said as he started to fill in the registration form with fictitious details.

'Suppose so, I'll need a week in advance.' Warren paid for two weeks up front.

'Third floor, number twelve.' Was all she said as she passed over the key, which was attached to a piece of plastic.

'Thanks, enjoy your day,' he replied sarcastically after the short transaction. She obviously wished she was somewhere else as she once again started work on her manicure.

Warren put the key in the door and turned the lock, he was quite surprised when he walked into the en-suite room. A double bed, large Ikea type wardrobe and dressing table, above all the room smelled clean and damp free. He threw his rucksack onto the bed and dropped down beside it. After unpacking his meagre belongings he had the same old problem – where to stash the Sig? Bottom of the wardrobe? Under the mattress? The room offered little in the way of places to conceal the weapon; he settled for the old option and removed the panel below the bath, wrapped the weapon in a towel, pushed it to the back and replaced the panel.

'Right, time for a visit,' he said to the empty room when the Sig was safely concealed. At the Priory Business Park, he parked the Fiesta well away from his final destination, he wanted to approach Gemmell Strategies discreetly, not in a noisy, highly tuned up Ford. From a distance nothing seemed to be out of the ordinary, the building looked the same as the last time he was there. The deep gravel of the car park crunched underfoot, glancing up he could see the security cameras on the front corners of the building. *Not much chance of surprise then*, he thought as he approached the doorway, expecting a voice to call out through the brass grill near the admittance button.

No voice, he pressed the bell, still no response and pressed again, this time keeping his finger on the button. Hammering on the door itself also proved to be no use. Then a voice came through the speaker grill. 'Can I help you?' Warren didn't recognise the voice.

'DS Greg Warren, open the door please,' Warren demanded reverting back to his old self.

'Sorry sir, the building is unoccupied at the moment.'

'Who am I speaking too?'

'Security sir, you have activated the remote sensors. Is there anything I can help you with?'

'Unoccupied, do you know when it *will be* occupied?'

'Sorry, sir, as far as we are aware they are on shut-down until further notice.'

What the hell is going on? 'Gemmell Strategies, do you have a contact number?'

'We do sir, but I can't give you it without verifying your identification.'

'Hang on a minute,' Warren took out his wallet and found the original business card Bob had given him. 'If I read out a couple of numbers, will you at least confirm if they're the same ones you hold?'

'I can live with that sir.' Warren read out the numbers and waited. 'Yes sir, that's the numbers we have.'

The more he thought about it, the more he was convinced Gemmell Strategies were responsible for his current predicament – he was an expendable resource. There was no reason as to why, only the fact that he had helped to put a very large amount of money into John and Bob's pension funds. Reason enough.

The drive back to the Shangri La was easy enough, traffic was light. He parked the Fiesta around the back of the hotel and used the rear door to enter. No sooner was he in his room than a text message came through. It was from Grimes. 'Need to meet urgent, same place, two hours.'

Warren was puzzled about what could be so urgent, there was nothing he could do to hurry the meeting, it was a question of being patient. He checked the Sig hadn't been tampered with then passed the time away with a shower and a change of clothes. Time was still dragging and Warren decided on a quick bottle of beer in the hotel bar, if you could call an ageing 1960s style cocktail bar in the corner of the lounge a bar.

Warren wasn't alone in the lounge, a tall, skinny balding bloke stood at the business side of the bar.

'Settled in alright?' Skinny asked.

'Yeah, thanks.'

'Staying long?'

'No, I shouldn't think so.'

'Not from around here then?'

'No.'

'So you're here on business then?'

'What's with the all the questions?' Warren snapped, not wanting to get drawn into conversation.

'Just being friendly that's all. What can I get you?'

'Tell you what, I've changed my mind,' he turned and walked from the lounge and out of the hotel. 'Nosey prat,' he said to himself as he walked down the concrete steps and headed towards the town centre. He checked his watch; there was still thirty minutes to go before the meeting. *A nice steady walk,* he told himself, periodically stopping and looking in shop windows, not browsing but checking he wasn't being tailed.

Grimes was already in the *Black Boy* when he arrived, a pint waiting for him on the table.

'Cheers,' Warren said as he sat down, 'what's so urgent?'

Grimes leaned in closer, elbows resting on the battle-scarred table top and keeping his voice low. 'Congratulations, your wanted status has just been upgraded to terrorism!'

'Oh for fuck's sake, how has that come about – terrorism?' Warren picked up his pint glass and swallowed half the contents in one go.

'Yeah well, you've been flagged up. Law enforcement agencies all over Europe are already interested in Cole's activities; it could be seen as natural progression. Anyway, I was checking out your mate the "real" Cole, and I got pinged and locked out of the system. Just a matter of time before someone asks what I was up to.'

'I'm really sorry about this Bill, the last thing I wanted was to drop you in the shit.'

'It seems someone wants you found pretty quick, can't think of a faster way to get your details out nationally. Probably be on *Crimewatch* tonight, then you'll be fucked.'

'Like I said, I didn't reckon on any of this mate.'

'Yeah well, it's too late now,' he said as he fumbled in his pocket for his e-cigarette. A little more relaxed with the faux cigarette in between his fingers, he sat back in his chair. 'Once I got pinged, I called a mate of mine in the Prison Service and asked him to make a few discreet enquiries. It seems Raymond Cole was topped, a couple of weeks back.'

'How?'

'Some con stuck him with a shiv, they found him dead in his cell.'

'Have they got the bloke that did him?'

'Some perv named Peter Price, doing life for sex offences against kids. Seems he had a gripe with Cole for cutting up his arse. Didn't have anything to lose – he was never getting out.'

'Think he was put up to it?'

'Seems logical. Probably doing some screw a good turn, in return for keeping him in baccy for the rest of his natural.'

'Gemmell would have the contacts to make that happen, I reckon that's why it's all been kept under wraps.'

'What the fuck have you got yourself into?'

'I keep asking myself the same question.'

'Did you find anything about Gemmell Strategies?'

'They're not registered with Companies House, but then we were expecting that. There's only so far I can go without dropping myself in it even further, the only useful info I've come across is they definitely run a "Black Operation", accountable only to the Home Office if truth be known I bet even the PM won't know they exist. One dangerous outfit.'

'Who told you this?' The conversation was making Warren even more paranoid; his head and neck constantly turning as he checked faces in the pub.

'An old mate of mine, he used to do some freelance work for the Intelligence Services.'

'You've got a lot of old mates.' The suspicion was raising.

'Lucky for you I have.'

'So, as I see it I'm right up shit creek.'

'Absolutely, up to your neck. You've no options left Greg, you have to let me take you in for your own safety.'

'Can't do that Bill, got to try and get to the bottom of this, why they were using me for their personal gain.'

Warren picked up a beer mat and unconsciously tore it into small pieces.

'Look Greg, I can have a word with the Super, tell him what's happened, we can protect you, it's the only way you'll be safe.'

'Like Cole you mean?' He said, looking up from the mess he had created. 'If they can get to him in High Security what chance would I have in a backwater nick? No thanks.'

'So, what's your next move?'

'My turn to ring a pal.'

'Anyone I know?'

'Well actually you do.' Warren smiled.

'Who?'

'Let's just say he's a mutual acquaintance and leave it at that.' Grimes wouldn't be very pleased if Warren told him he was going to call Conway.

'It seems to me it's just a matter of time before they put your real name out there. A rogue copper with an automatic gun on the streets – there'll be a hue and cry.'

'Have to keep my head down and try to get this mess sorted.'

'The good thing is you look a bloody mess, not like the photograph they're likely to put out.' Grimes stood up to leave. 'If you need me you know where I am, just keep your head down.'

'Thanks Bill, I'll be in touch.'

Warren wandered over to the bar, ordered single malt and returned to the table alone. As he sipped, he studied the faces of the punters, of course no one was interested in him, but he was suspicious of every face. If he was to come through this in one piece he needed access to Gemmell Strategies files.

Warren didn't notice the smart businessman wearing a two-piece charcoal grey suit, standing at the far end of the bar, checking his iPad and who occasionally looked into the mirror behind the optics, observing. Although Warren was a professional, this guy was good, he was better.

Staples had been in the 'game' a long time, too long he was always telling himself. Once he had shown he was prepared to do anything asked of him, regardless of the legitimacy, his association with Gemmell Strategies had proved to be very lucrative. He knew he was coming to the end of his tenure with the organisation, and planned to retire to a sunnier climate sooner rather than later. Terminating Warren was to be his 'swan song'.

Shadowing someone was the easy part of the job – he had had years of practise. He had no problems in discreetly following Warren through the town centre, back to the Shangri La. Although Warren had removed the tracking device from under the bonnet of the Fiesta, he hadn't banked on there being two devices. The second had been concealed inside of the rear bumper, running on an independent power supply; every move the Fiesta made was recorded on Staples's iPad.

He made the reverse journey to the Shangri La, again with the occasional glance over his shoulder and checking in windows. 'Give it up for fuck's sake, Bill's right you're paranoid,' he said to himself as he saw his reflection in a phone shop window. 'Little Miss I Couldn't Give A Toss', was on duty when he walked into the hotel foyer. From the snide look she gave him he reckoned the skinny bloke must have told her what had happened, not that anything really did, but the story was probably embellished beyond recognition.

From the shelter of a disused shop doorway Staples watched Warren enter the hotel. He waited a while, giving him time enough to reach his room. Then Staples crossed the busy road, up the concrete steps and walked into the hotel foyer, nodded to the girl and went to his own room. It hadn't been hard to persuade the girl on the reception to give him the room next to Warren, once two fifty pound notes were placed in front of her.

Chapter 25

In his own room Warren did what he always did first, check the Sig was still in place. Leaving the panel loose, he took the weapon through to the bedroom, wondering if he was ever likely to use it. He sat in the only chair and prayed the answer would remain no. He laid the holstered weapon on the bed and took out the second mobile, changed the SIM card and called Conway.

'I wondered when you'd surface. Where the fuck did you disappear to?' he demanded to know.

'Doesn't really matter where I am.'

'You got my gear back?'

'Working on it, that's why I'm calling – need to borrow Jimbo for a couple of days.'

'Time's running out Ray, I can't wait forever… know what I mean?'

'Look, give me a break, can I have Jimbo or don't you want your money?'

'Break? I'll break your fucking neck. Yes, you can have him, just get what's mine, sharpish.'

Warren smiled, finished the call and dialled Jimbo's number.

'Jimbo, how's the head?' He didn't wait for the reply. 'Fancy earning some beer money?'

'No thanks I'm busy. If I remember rightly, the last time I worked with you things didn't exactly go as planned, *and* I had my head caved in.'

'Yeah, well, I'm sorry about that, look I need someone I can trust – I'll make it worth your while, what do you reckon?' Warren said, trying to cajole Jimbo into accepting.

'Am I likely to get bashed again?'

'Can't lie to you Jimbo it's more likely than not. What do you say?'

'When?'

'Good man, what are you doing tonight?'

'Seems I'm working with you. Must need my fuckin' head looked at – again.'

'Cheers pal, I'm staying at the Shangri La on Springbank.'

'Bloody hell, you really know how to live the high life, staying in that dump. What is it you want me to do?'

'It's a long story, the short version goes something like this…'

Warren's stomach thought his throat had been cut. He hadn't eaten since his greasy breakfast in the hotel's lounge-cum-breakfast-room. In light of what Grimes had told him, he didn't fancy being too far away from the hotel in daylight hours, he decided the best option was to keep a low profile. His only option to eat was a burger bar 200 metres down from the *Shangri La*. With more greasy food in front of him, a double cheeseburger and fries, he was considering the feasibility of his next move, a night time visit to Gemmell Strategies. His mobile vibrated on the table next to his coffee. He picked it up, recognised the caller displayed and pressed the accept key.

'You do know there's some bloke tailing you?'

Across the road from the burger bar, *browsing* at the goods offered for sale in a charity shop, Jimbo was doing as instructed, watching Warren's back.

'If I'd known that I wouldn't have to pay you,' he replied light-heartedly.

'He was thirty seconds behind you coming out of the hotel – mind you he's good.'

'He came out of the Shangri La?'

'Yep, hot on your heels.'

'What's he look like?'

'Smart bloke, sharp suit, collar length hair combed back, I reckon he's around thirty, thirty-five. You know him?'

'Can't say I do, keep an eye on him.'

'That's what you're paying me for.'

The cogs turned around in Warren's brain. If he was a cop they would have picked him up by now, the alternative, which didn't bear thinking about he was one of Gemmell's men.

'I've been careful, can't work out how whoever he is found me. You reckon on him coming in here?'

'Only if you stop in there too long, I reckon he might come to have a 'look-see'.'

'Ok, I'll slip the waiter a tenner and come out through the service door, reckon you can delay him if he heads this way?'

'No problem, hey up I think he's thinking about moving, didn't think he'd be that quick. Where's the car?'

'Car park back of the hotel, I'll meet you there.'

Warren stood up casually and walked across to the counter to pay the bill, adding a ten-pound tip and nodding towards the kitchen. The waiter smiled, pocketed the note and stood aside to let Warren pass. He looked over his shoulder to see Jimbo taking up position, that of a dosser begging in the doorway.

Jimbo played the aggressive beggar, sitting on the floor in front of the entrance to the burger restaurant. 'Giz a quid mate,' he said as Staples approached.

'Fuck off.' He expected Jimbo to move.

'Fifty pence then,' he edged further in blocking the doorway completely.

'Tell you what I will give you – a fucking good kicking if you don't move.' Staples took half a step forward until his feet were touching Jimbo.

Slowly, very slowly Jimbo moved away. 'Bastard,' he said to Staples back.

Staples hesitated, wondering whether to turn and give him a kicking anyway, thought better of it and opened the door and went inside. He stood looking around, there was no sign of Warren. 'Bloke who was in here, where is he?'

The waiter shrugged his shoulder, all the man had to do was cross his palm with silver and he'd have told him.

Warren had gained an extra three or four minutes. As soon as Staples was in the door, Jimbo leapt to his feet and legged it down Springbank. Ten minutes later they were heading down towards the Hessle Foreshore in the Fiesta.

'Don't know how the fucker found me.'

'Who is he?'

'Take your pick, maybe a cop, he could be being paid by someone I upset while I was in the nick, and there was a few of them. On the other hand, he could be the bloke we ran into on the *Seabird.*'

'That's it!' Jimbo exclaimed. 'His aftershave, I thought I recognised it, he's the fucker who bashed me head in.'

Brilliant, that's all I need now, some fucker putting a hit on me. You reckon he could have recognised you?'

'I wouldn't say so, the day he clobbered me he came at me from the back, never clocked me face.'

Warren pulled up the Fiesta below the towers of the Humber Bridge and both men climbed out of the low sprung car.

'Might be fast but it's not very comfortable,' grumbled Jimbo as he stretched his long legs.

Warren ignored him and walked across to the river's edge, staring across to Barton on the far side. He turned to face the young man, the man who for some strange reason he trusted.

'Look Jimbo if this bloke's after topping me, then I reckon you could be putting yourself on the line. I've changed my mind and want you to walk away. No hard feelings and all that.'

'Yeah like fuck, what are mates for?'

'I don't want to be visiting you in the Infirmary – or the cemetery.'

'Like you mean me cousin?'

'He's dead?' Warren asked, seriously.

'No, the Infirmary.' He seemed to have enjoyed seeing the worried look on Warren's face.

'Sorry about that, but it was either him or me.'

'Yeah, he told me, he'd have done you if you hadn't got in first. Water under the bridge and all that,' then laughed when he realised where they were standing – directly under the Humber Bridge.

'If you insist on hanging around I'll make sure you get a good pay day out of it.'

'Whatever, give us the car keys.' Warren passed them over. 'Let's see if they put a tracker on the car.'

'Already been over it, you won't find one.'

He stood to aside and watched Jimbo work. Bonnet opened and every inch of the engine space was inspected, nothing, as Warren expected. Next the younger man was doubled in the foot-well of the car checking under the dashboard, nothing.

'Can't work it out,' Jimbo said, 'got to be somewhere, how else did he know where you were?' He stood back with his hands in his pockets as the wind blew in gusts off the river. 'Unless,' he said as he walked around the front, dropped to his knees and reached under the car, arm bent at the elbow he felt the full length of the inside of the bumper, nothing. Not saying anything, he stood up and walked around to rear, again he dropped down and lay on his back and shuffled underneath, there it was, a twinkling blue light between the petrol tank and the underside of the Fiesta. 'Got ya, ya fucker,' he said as he yanked it free and separated the wires to prevent a short circuit. Still on his back he shuffled out. 'There you go Ray,' he said as he stood up and tossed the tracking device to Warren.

'Good man, never thought about under there.'

'That's because you're a "proper" crim not a common thief like me.' He took the tracking unit back and threw it as far as he could into the river.

'Come on, there's something I've got to do.'

Back in the tracker-free Fiesta, Warren drove to Gemmell Strategies on the Priory Park Business site, a matter of minutes away. He pulled up some 200 metres away.

'What we doing here?' Asked Jimbo.

'That office over there,' he pointed towards Gemmell Strategies. 'I need to be inside, reckon you can get me in?' Jimbo didn't answer, just gave Warren one of those 'looks'.

'The security is pretty good, no it's more than good, it's first-rate.'

'Ray, you do ask some stupid questions.' Both men laughed.

'There's an on-site security office with a couple of numpties in charge, the bigger problem is that the alarm system is linked to the security's main office and the police.'

'Ok, that just means we've got to use our noddles. Can we take a look?'

Warren slipped the Fiesta into gear and did a steady drive past, not too fast, not too slow as to arouse suspicion, twice around the block as if they were looking for a particular address.

'Right,' said Jimbo 'the way I see it we'll have to go in from the roof.'

'The roof?'

'Yeah, notice most of the snoopy cameras are on the front of the building? They're covering the car park and there's a couple on the sides, but 'cos there's no windows round the back they're aimed down the sides of the building towards the front. Now the rear of the building is a different kettle of fish, no doors, no windows with a two-metre service gap between them and the building they back onto. And guess what?'

'No cameras?'

'Yep, and even better it doesn't look occupied, if I'm right and it's not there's more than an even money chance their surveillance cameras won't be working.'

'Any way we can check?'

'Not without dropping ourselves in it, but my guess is they won't be working, what's to guard? Bugger all, the place looks as if it's been shut down for months, they won't want to pay for security to guard fuck all. Take us for a drive around to check it out.'

'So how does it work getting in through the roof?'

'Air-con, no units on side of the building so it stands to reason they're on the roof.' Warren was surprised, for such a young bloke Jimbo was a fountain of knowledge when it came to breaking and entering. 'Also no fire escape ladder on outside of the building, so my guess is there's got to be some hatch on the roof to let the engineers service the air-con units.'

'What if there's no hatch?'

'We unfasten a few bolts, move the unit and we're halfway there, open the hole up a bit, then we're in the roof-space, kick out the ceiling and we're in.'

'As easy as that?'

'Yeah well, sounds easy, but the bigger problem will be once we've gained access, we won't know what cameras or sensors there are inside. Cameras, ok we can deal with them with a bit of spray paint on the lenses, won't give us long, only minutes till security notices they've been blacked out so you'll have to work fast.'

'The sensors?' asked Warren.

'Just have to take a chance and be ready to do a runner. When do you want to do this?'

'Sooner rather than later – tomorrow night?'

'Ok, that'll give me time to sort some gear out.'

'In the meantime, this bloke who was tailing me, let's see what that's all about. But first, you fancy a burger?'

Warren drove to the McDonald's Drive Thru on St Andrews Quay. Armed with paper bags of burgers and fries, they sat in the parking area near the *Sailmakers* pub. Warren put his paper package on the dashboard top.

'Just give me a minute will you,' he climbed from the Fiesta, took out his mobile and walked around the back of the car, holding the phone close to his ear. 'It's me,' he said into the receiver. The call was to Inspector Bill Grimes. 'Do you know if there's a tail on me?'

'Not as far as I'm aware, why what's happened?'

'Looks like my acquaintance from the yacht might have me in his sights.'

'Any idea who it is?'

'Working on it.'

'What can I do?'

'Nothing yet, just wanted to be sure. Cheers mate.' He hung up and returned to the car.

'Gonna tell me who it was?' Jimbo asked as he got back in the car.

'You really don't want to know Jimbo and that's the truth. The top and bottom of it is it's not the police tailing me. Reckon it's time I moved on from the *Shangri La*.'

'You can sleep on my settee if you want,' Jimbo offered.

'Are you sure mate? The way things are going it's not looking too good and I don't want to bring more trouble to your doorstep.'

'What are mates for? Let's go get your stuff.'

Chapter 26

There was no problem checking out of the hotel as he'd already paid up front. All he had to do was collect the Sig and his belongings and walk away.

But he had something to do first.

'Anyone been asking about me?' he asked 'Miss Couldn't Give A Toss I'm Doing My Nails', on the reception of the *Shangri La*. Warren took out his wallet and opened it so the contents were clearly visible and lay it flat on the desk top. He took out a twenty and placed it on the desk. Miss Disinterested looked at the money and back to Warren, holding his gaze. Another twenty was placed with the first, still she kept her gaze. 'Alright, you win,' said Warren as he picked up his wallet and counted a further sixty pounds.

'Now you mention it, there was a man asking about someone who fitted your description, he even booked a room.'

'What room is he in?'

'Fourteen, the room next to yours.'

'Name?'

She flicked through the registration cards. 'He's booked in under the name G. Emmell.'

Warren smiled. 'Is he in?'

'No, not at the moment.'

'Do you have any idea what kind of car he drives?' She looked into his eyes again and smiled.

'It's a dark blue BMW.'

He took a further two twenty pound notes out of his wallet and put it with the one hundred already on the desk. He didn't have to say anything else, she reached under the desk and handed him a master key.

With the key in his hand Warren took the stairs two at a time. The corridor was empty, but then again, even if anyone saw him it would appear as if he was going into his own room, after all, he *was* using a key. Outside room fifteen he stood and listened. No sound. He put the key in the lock and turned, still no sound from inside. Now with no need for caution he opened the door quickly, entered and closed the door behind him.

The layout of the room was pretty much the same as his own, standard Ikea furniture and fittings. *So who are you?* he whispered, the room looked almost unused, no sign of anything personal was on view. Warren opened the bedside cupboard drawer, nothing but the standard Gideon Bible. A search of the wardrobe and drawers revealed about as much, a couple of shirts, socks and underwear. There was nothing in the room to give an identity to the man who had been following him. Just the trapping of a man used to travelling light. Finding a laptop or PDA would have been too much to ask. He thought about removing the bath panel, as he knew that was the most secure place to temporarily leave anything valuable or incriminating but he was pushing his luck, time was against him. He made sure everything was as he'd found it, double checked and then quietly left the room and locked the door. In his own room he removed the Sig from the bathroom, placed it in the bottom of the rucksack and covered it with his meagre belongings – he wasn't coming back.

In the reception area he dropped the master key on the desk. Little Miss I Couldn't Give A Toss didn't even raise her head, she was probably already planning what to spend the one hundred pounds on.

'Have you a sheet of paper and an envelope, please?' he asked.

She reached under the desk, opened a drawer then passed the paper and envelope across. Warren picked up a pen off the desk and wrote a quick note. 'Be seeing you soon, be lucky', placed it in the envelope and sealed it, and scribbled 'Room 15'.

'When he comes back give him this will you?'

Warren smiled to himself as he walked out of the hotel. He was looking forward to the meeting.

'You took your time,' Jimbo said as Warren open the car door.

'I've just been on a recce, the cheeky bastard following me had the room next to mine. Let's pay a visit to the "offy" and get a couple of bottles,' he said, as they drove away. 'You think you can lay your hand on a GPS tracking unit?'

'Yeah, but not until the morning.'

'That'll do nicely.'

Back in Jimbo's living room, Warren filled him in on the details of his search of the 'tail's' room. and they discussed what he intended to do with the tracking unit, attach it to the BMW, and turn things around to their advantage.

Chapter 27

'We'll stand out like a couple of spare pricks on that roof in this moonlight,' Jimbo grumbled.

Warren looked at his watch, it was 1.30am. They had been in the service gap at the rear of Gemmell Strategies for the past two hours, gradually getting colder in the near-freezing temperature as they waited for the moon to disappear behind the clouds, before risking their necks climbing the plastic service pipe to the roof.

'Where's the bleedin' clouds?'

'Won't be long now.'

'Hope not, I'm freezing me bollocks off.'

'Not being funny Jimbo, that pipe might take the weight of a skinny fella like you, but I don't reckon I'll get very far before it comes away.'

'Thought about that, that's why I brought this,' he produced a heavy-duty nylon line from his backpack. 'I'll shimmy up and drop you a line.'

'You'll never take my weight!' Warren protested.

'I'll fasten it off somewhere, if not you'll have to take the risk I can hold you.'

'Couldn't you get anything a bit stronger?'

'Stop whining Ray, it'll be fine.'

The younger man was really enjoying seeing the hard-man squirm.

'That'll be all I need on top of everything else – a couple of broken legs.'

A large cloud started to cover the bright moon. Both men put on tight fitting leather gloves.

'See you on the roof old man,' said Jimbo as he put on his backpack and started his climb.

'Unfortunately,' muttered Warren, not relishing the thought of trusting his weight to a length of nylon rope not much thicker than a clothesline. It was only a matter of a few minutes before the nylon rope was dangling down the side of the two-storey building. 'Here goes,' Warren said under his breath as he firmly grabbed the rope and gave it a couple of good tugs. A face appeared over the edge of the flat roof, smiling. He began to climb, hand over hand, the rope held tight not giving an inch. Jimbo had tied the rope off around the collar of the roof hatch. The muscles in Warren's arms were burning, and his knees were well bashed about by the time he stuck his head over the roof edge.

'Took your time,' Jimbo taunted as Warren heaved himself over the edge and lay on the flat roof, breathing as if he'd just run a marathon race. 'Not very fit are you Ray, thought you blokes in the nick worked on the weights in the gym?'

'Piss off... how do we get in?' he asked between breaths.

'Well in the time it took you to shimmy up the wall I found us a way in. Like I reckoned there's a service hatch. Might have all the hi-tech security down below, but they usually scrimp a bit on the roof. The hatch is fitted with a two-way cylinder dead bolt; by two-way I mean it can be opened from the inside or good news for us, the outside.' Jimbo fished about in the backpack he'd put down next to the hatch and took out a steel 'dolly', a metal bar six inches long and three quarters of an inch in diameter. Next he produced a rubber coated steel mallet. 'Watch and learn.' He placed the bar onto the cylinder, holding it with his left hand, mallet in his right he struck down hard on the bar with hardly a sound, once, twice then there was the sound of the cylinder falling to the floor inside the building. 'That's it.'

He put down the mallet and the 'dolly', put his fingertips under the edge of the fibreglass lid and lifted. The hydraulic ram attached to the lid made the opening effortless as he eased it back on its hinges.

'Bloody hell Jimbo, you never stop surprising me,' said Warren, as he turned on his mini-torch and peered into the void, expecting to hear the shrill of the alarm. Silence. He looked to Jimbo and smiled, then leaned in the hatchway and released the expanding ladder. Crash – the ladder unfolded with an unearthly rattle until it reached the floor, still no alarm sounded. As quietly as he could he descended down the aluminium rungs. Jimbo followed.

'You been in here before?' asked Jimbo.

'Yep,' said Warren as he stood scanning around for CCTV cameras.

'Do you know where the alarm panel is?'

'Ground floor in the foyer, why?'

'Just got a feeling.'

'Come on Jimbo, you can do better than that.'

'We've just broken into what you reckon is a high security building through the roof, dropped a metal fucking ladder eight feet to the floor, and still the alarm didn't go off!'

'You worry too much,' said Warren, but underneath he agreed with what Jimbo said. As far as he could remember he was sure there weren't any cameras on the stairwell. Nevertheless, he cautiously led the way down to the foyer. 'Over there,' he said inclining his head towards the alarm panel. Jimbo threw caution to wind and headed directly into the centre of the reception area. 'What the fuck are you doing – the cameras?'

Jimbo stood looking up at the multi-directional dome camera in the centre of the ceiling, then towards Warren, and the confidently strode across to the alarm cabinet and shone his torch's beam on the panel door. 'Ray, come and see this,' he said as he opened the metal door. 'Not even fucking locked.'

Warren could feel the sweat running down the centre of his back; he was still expecting the alarm to sound. Reluctantly, he walked over to Jimbo. 'What the hell?' he said, 'never mind locked, it's not even fucking turned on!'

'Are you sure this place is occupied?' questioned Jimbo.

'One hundred per cent, I used to…' he faltered, 'have dealings with the people who own it.'

'Well, I reckon you should get on with looking for whatever we came for.'

Warren left Jimbo looking around for whatever he thought he could nick and sell on, while he went straight to the main office. Everything was pretty much the same as the last time he'd visited. He wasn't surprised that all the filing cabinets containing the personnel files were locked. He was surprised that the safe door was wide open.

'I don't believe this,' he said aloud to himself. The safe had been emptied, barring two files that lay as if waiting for him, side by side. One was his own and another belonging to Peter Staples. 'You devious bastards,' again he spoke out aloud. 'You were expecting me, too much to have expected the diamonds to be here.' Warren took the files and tucked them inside his jacket. 'Done here Jimbo,' he said wondering who the hell Peter Staples could be. The shooter from the yacht?

'Yep, so am I,' Jimbo came in with his backpack over his shoulder, now even heavier due to the two laptop computers on their way to new homes.

Jimbo started back up the stairwell. 'Hang on,' said Warren, 'what's the point of shimmying down that rope when we can walk out of the front door?'

'Point taken.'

Jimbo took off the backpack, opened it up and took out a short, steel nail bar, he hooked the claw end between the door and frame and levered. As the door sprung open, Warren managed to catch it before it swung back on itself, preventing even more noise. Jimbo stuck his head out of the door, all quiet, and led the way around the side of the building to where they had cut the wire fence to gain access to the service gap.

'Get what you wanted?' asked Jimbo when they were back in the Fiesta. When Warren didn't rely he repeated the question.

'Sorry Jimbo, I was miles away,' replied Warren, who had been lost in thought for a few minutes. 'Yeah I did.'

'Didn't do too bad myself,' he said as he reached over and put the backpack into the rear.

'As a professional thief what's your take on the fact all the alarms were turned off?' he asked Jimbo.

'Does make you wonder, I mean, you said to expect hi-tech security. Maybe we should be grateful and shouldn't look a gift horse in the mouth?'

'Yes, but surely it was too easy, it was as if we – I was expected. Maybe you'd better dump the laptops mate. Probably have GPS installed; they could be tracking us right now.'

'Or we could give them what they want, if they want to follow someone, let's give them someone to follow if you get my drift.'

'Oh yes I get your drift alright. Where shall we send it?' he said as he put the car into gear and drove away from the business park.

'I don't know, just find a lorry and send it on its way.'

They did a tour of the Hessle Road industrial area searching for a suitable vehicle. They found it parked up along Havelock Street. Warren pulled into the kerbside. 'That'll do,' he nodded to the purple liveried curtain-sided lorry. The driver was at the front of the vehicle messing with the off-side front wheel and he'd left the vehicle with its engine running.

Jimbo reached into the back and grabbed the backpack. He opened the door and climbed out, then casually walked to the blind side of the vehicle, eased the loose curtain to a side and threw in the backpack. He stood back and read the sign writing on the canvas and smiled.

'Where's it going?' Warren asked as Jimbo took up his seat.

'Bruges, probably be on the ferry in a couple of hours.'

'Well if the GPS *is* activated that'll keep them guessing for while, bloody Belgium. I like it.'

Twenty minutes later they were in Jimbo's living room, slowly getting pissed. Not that it took a lot of alcohol for the booze to take effect, it had been a busy day and they were both knackered.

'Here's to a good night's work, cheers.' Warren saluted with his glass of malt, he'd given up the pretence with the tequila.

'Yeah it wasn't so bad, at least nobody bashed me on the head this time,' said Jimbo as he saluted back with his tinnie. 'You having another Ray?' He pointed to the near empty glass.

'No thanks pal, think it's time I got my head down.'

'No stamina old man,' Jimbo quipped as he headed off to the only bedroom.

Warren placed a cushion against the padded arm of the settee, finished his malt and placed the glass on the floor. 'Goodnight Jimbo.' He kicked off his shoes, lifted his legs onto the settee and stretched out, resting his head back on the soft cushion. Sleep came quickly.

Chapter 28

Warren woke early with a crick in his back from the soggy settee springs. He could hear Jimbo snoring like a trooper through the closed bedroom door. He smiled, the lad had turned out to be a trusted friend. Warren spun his legs around, reached around and massaged the small of his back. Quietly as he could, trying not to disturb his host he went through to the kitchen, filled and turned on the kettle then returned to the tap and splashed his face with cold water. He was in need of an urgent caffeine fix. He needed a clear head when he read the files he'd hidden under the settee cushions. Warren sat back on the settee with his feet up on the coffee table and sipped the hot mug of cheap supermarket blend instant coffee. He picked up the files, had a quick glance through his own, which strangely enough he found was mostly complimentary. The file he was really interested in was that belonging to Peter Staples, it wasn't the original and looked like a copy.

Peter Staples had a coloured past, aged thirty-six, an ex-member of the Parachute Regiment with tours of Afghanistan and Iraq under his belt before being accepted into the 'Regiment', where he served a further two years as a Sergeant in the SAS. An expert linguist, he was well suited to interrogation work and was an experienced field operative, often working deep undercover for weeks on end. On completion of his term with the 'Regiment; he'd been headhunted by Gemmell Strategies, an association that began four years ago and was still ongoing.

The rest of the file was sketchy. Several pages were missing, but it still made interesting reading. Staples had been involved in a number of their covert operations, the details of which had been scrubbed through with a black marker pen, to be expected. But as it said on the front of the file he was 'Active', leading him to believe Staples to be responsible for the hit on the *Seabird*. Warren was puzzled; he couldn't work out why they had left a confidential file for him to just pick up? Obviously they wanted Warren to know, but why?

He tucked the folders back under the cushions as Jimbo emerged from the bedroom wearing just his boxer shorts. 'You're up early,' he said, as he stretched his arms above his head, yawning.

'Another busy day ahead, you're going to sort me out some tracking gear, remember?'

'Give us a chance Ray, let me have a coffee and a scratch first!' he called from the kitchen above the noise of the kettle boiling. 'Anyway, the bloke who has 'em only lives down the road. You want a brew?'

Jimbo came through to the living room carrying two chipped mugs of coffee and set them down on the coffee table and picked up the television remote.

'You haven't got time for breakfast telly.'

'I always watch while I have my coffee and come round a bit, anyway you stink! No offence like, but you do.' Warren couldn't argue with that one. 'You can use the shower while I watch me telly then we can get sorted.'

'Piss off Jimbo,' he made the pretence of sniffing under his arms. 'Maybe you're right. Be ready to go when I come out,' he grabbed his wash bag and headed for Jimbo's tiny but clean shower.

'Yeah, yeah, whatever.' If the truth was known, Jimbo very rarely watched any television at all, never mind the early morning crap, he was subtly setting his rules – he was the boss in his own home and they'd go for breakfast when *he* was ready.

'I was ready for this,' Warren said as they tucked into their 'builders' breakfasts', a pile of greasy sausages, eggs, bacon and the trimmings, along with two steaming mugs of tea.

'Billy always does a good breakfast for his regulars, I start most of me days in here,' he said as he forked half a sausage into his mouth.

'Has Conway been keeping tabs on us?'

'Nah, he's sweet, not heard a word. Mind you I don't know how long his patience will last, I reckon he's too busy trying to keep Big Jim happy. Do you reckon you can get his gear back?'

'To be truthful with you Jimbo I don't know, I'd be lying if I said yes. I can try and I'm partial to walking on two legs, so I'll do my best.'

'Hope your best is good enough mate – know what I mean?'
More sausage and bacon went down the hatch.

'So, how does this tracker work?' Warren had eaten enough and pushed away his plate.

'Got your mobile?' Jimbo put down his knife and fork and held out his hand. Warren passed over the Nokia. 'You're kidding me right? This ain't no fucking good on the internet. We'll have to get you something decent, till we get that sorted we'll use mine.'

Jimbo pushed aside his breakfast, took out his all-singing, all-dancing mobile and tapped in the http address and a password. 'This is the screen we'll see, once we put the device on the BMW it will show like this.' He pointed to the various coloured dots on the screen.

'How come all these vehicles are already on there?'

'Cos the site belongs to my mate, he monitors it for a car-hire company in case any get nicked. We're just borrowing a bit of space and going on his system,' he disconnected the phone from the server and put it back in his pocket. 'You fit then?' he said, as he finished his mug of tea and stood up waiting for Warren.

They left the Fiesta parked partially concealed from view between a Transit van and a Renault people carrier in the car park of the Iceland store on Springbank. The Shangri La was a couple of streets away. A quick check of the car park revealed Staples's BMW was still there. Warren knew it wasn't visible from room fifteen at the front of the building. Standing in the hotel's rear doorway he kept watch, as Jimbo nonchalantly walked over to the BMW and made a show of tying the lace of his trainer. As he stood up, he reached under the front wheel arch, he felt the pull as the tracker attached itself to the metalwork. He made the pretence of brushing himself down and casually walked out of the car park, Warren hot on his heels.

'Piece of piss,' said Jimbo to Warren walking closely behind him.

'A pint in *The Eagle*?'

'If you're buying – see you in there,' he said, as he crossed the main road, leaving Warren to walk on.

Chapter 29

'Hello again,' the girl behind the bar said to Warren. 'Foster's?'

'You've got a good memory for faces,' he said, as he leaned on the bar.

'Only for the nice looking ones,' she flirted.

Warren smiled. 'Best make that two pints please.' He placed a ten pound note on the bar top. 'Keep the change.'

'Thanks very much, I'll bring them over.

Sat in the bar of *The Eagle*, two pints in, Jimbo had his iPhone out on the table. The atmosphere was tense as they waited and watched for Staples's BMW to make a move. Warren could sense Jimbo wasn't his usual self, instead quiet and sullen.

'You got a problem Jimbo, something bothering you?' Warren pushed a packet of dry roasted nuts across the table.

'Nope. Nowt bothering me,' he lied, pushing the packet back. Jimbo sat back in his chair with his arms folded across his chest, staring Warren in the eyes.

'If *nowt's* bothering you, then why have you got a face like a slapped arse?'

Jimbo tried to ignore him, but couldn't. He sat forward and rested his elbows on the table. 'Can I ask you something?' His face a mask of seriousness.

'You know you can.'

'Who the fuck *are* you?'

'What sort of question is that? You know who I am.' Warren guessed what was coming.

'I know who you *say* you are and who Mick *thinks* you are. Me – I think there's a bit more to it.'

'Like what?'

'One minute you're a super cool top villain, the next minute you're – I don't know you go all strange on me and act like a copper. So which are you?'

Warren turned to face his young friend. 'What makes you ask a question like that?'

'Like I said, don't really know, something about you just doesn't add up. These people you reckon are after you, tracking systems, the discreet phone calls – it's all seems a bit secret squirrel to me.'

'Seriously, there's nothing for you to worry about, finish your beer.'

'Don't get me wrong, I think you're a top bloke, but I need to know.' Jimbo was almost pleading to know the truth.

'I think we'd better have another pint don't you?'

Warren went to the bar and came back with two pints of lager and a couple of whisky chasers. He knew it would only have been a matter of time before the lad started to question things – Jimbo wasn't thick. It was the law of averages. Sooner or later he would be sussed; he just hoped it would have been later. The silence dragged on for a couple of minutes, he didn't know how to start the conversation without freaking Jimbo out.

'My name is Greg Warren, and I'm a Sergeant with Humberside Police…'

'I knew it, I fucking knew it!' Almost standing up as he banged his fists on the table rattling the glasses.

'Hang on a minute before you get all uppity on me, I was a police officer, maybe I still am. I'm not quite sure whether I'm a copper or a villain.'

'After all I've done for you and you drop this on me. Wanker.'

'I thought you just said I was a top bloke?' he tried hard to smile, not succeeding in keeping things on the light side.

'Yeah well, like you *I'm* not sure anymore.' Jimbo picked up his whisky and knocked it back in one. 'I took a fucking good hiding for you!' He sat back folding his arms once more. 'Wanker,' he said again bitterly staring Warren in the eye.

The silence settled around them, both waiting for the other to speak.

'From what they tell me I was a dead ringer for the real Ray Cole, a bloody double, that's how all this came about.'

Jimbo was quick picking up on the *was*. 'Was – what happened to him?'

'Cole was being held on some trumped up charge in Belmarsh. The escape, my so-called escape was all staged for the media. I didn't take part and the real Cole didn't know what was going on. Cole was given the shiv, died in Belmarsh, they told me he was topped by some nonce he'd had a run-in with. If you ask me, it was more than likely a put-up job, I reckon they thought it would clear the way for whatever operation they had in mind for me.'

He picked up a pint and wet his dry throat.

'The idea was for me to go "deep" undercover. It was supposed to be a long operation, maybe months or more. The plan was for me to infiltrate Conway's operation at ground level and see where it led. We were hoping it would have led further up the chain. It was supposed to be a long haul, but it wasn't to be, the diamonds came along and my bosses got too greedy. I think they saw it as too good an opportunity to miss.'

'Would you have nicked Mick?'

'Eventually.'

'And me?'

'Probably.'

'Fuck.'

'Things have changed Jimbo, I'm not the same person. Let's face it, the people who employed me have disowned me – they want me topped.'

Jimbo was silent; he didn't know how to handle the situation.

'I'm listening,' was all he said.

'There's not a lot left to say. The tables have been turned against me. I've got Conway on my back wanting his gear, the cops have me down as a terrorist and I've got a price on my head, which brings us to Staples who wants to blow my fucking brains out.

What happens next has a lot to do with you. The way I see it you can give Conway a call and drop me in the shit or maybe we could call at the nick on the way home and I could hand myself in. I won't try and stop you either way, it's your call.'

'Fucking hell, you really know how to guilt trip a bloke.'

Jimbo was stuck between a rock and a hard place

'That wasn't what I was trying to do, just making your options clear. As I said, it's up to you what happens next.'

'Fuck this,' he stood up almost pushing the table over and walked away, Warren was half expecting him to walk out of the door and was surprised when he went to the bar.

Warren remained sitting at the table. Jimbo turned, looked at him and shook his head in disbelief. He'd had an inkling something wasn't as it should be; now it was confirmed, only worse than he thought. The bloke who he'd trusted with his life and let sleep on his settee – a copper. Jimbo returned and put down two pints on the table.

'So what's it to be?' Warren asked as Jimbo sat down.

'Fucked if I know, still thinking about it. If I decide not to drop you in it with Mick what's the next move?'

'I genuinely do want to try and get Conway his gear back but right now my priority is keeping alive. Staples missed his chance on the *Seabird*, but the truth would be more like he was only paid for the two executions; he wasn't going to give them a freebie.'

Jimbo had got over his initial shock. 'So, what's our plan?'

'Our plan?'

'Yeah well, for now anyway, I can always change my mind.'

Warren relaxed, picked up his drink and sipped, put down the glass and looked Jimbo directly in the eye.

'The way I see it is this – we have to turn the tables to our advantage and be proactive. If we – I, sit back and do nothing I'll end up on the slab like the real Cole.'

'So what you're telling me is, we've got to top this bloke Staples?'

'In a nutshell, yes.'

'Any ideas how we gonna do this? 'Cos if he tops *you* first I won't get paid and you owe me a fucking fortune already.'

Warren was quick in noticing the "we" and smiled.

'Jimbo, if I make it out of this mess I'll make sure you get paid with a hefty bonus. For now, we've got to be patient, its watch and wait time. For once we have the advantage,' he tapped Jimbo's iPhone. 'We'll be ready when the time comes. In the meantime, while we sit here and get pissed why don't you tell me a bit about yourself?'

'Not much to tell really.'

'Mick told me about your mam being in that home.'

'Yeah well, he had no fucking business. Anyway, what should I be calling you now?' His life so far hadn't been much to talk about and for now he preferred to keep it to himself.

Warren turned and smiled. 'Anything you like as long as it doesn't rhyme with hunt.'

'Greg Warren, Raymond Cole, Sergeant – think I'll stick with Ray, at least until this is over.'

Chapter 30

'Be careful,' John remarked as the site security people trudged through the building, making the roof access secure. 'Very resourceful,' he said, as he stood looking up at the roof hatch.

'Who's resourceful?'

'The young man Warren's teamed up with.' He examined the roof hatch lock tumbler. 'He appears to be quite capable.'

'Perhaps we should invite him to join us when this fiasco is over?'

John raised his eyebrows at the suggestion. 'Have you heard anything from Peter?'

'Not since our meeting.'

'Chase him up will you?'

Chapter 31

'We've been stuck in this flat since we got back last night,' Jimbo looked at his watch, 7pm. 'Nearly eighteen hours! Any chance we can get out for a while?'

'It's not worth the risk, won't be much longer I'm sure of it,' Warren called into the kitchen where Jimbo was making fried egg on toast.

Warren had had his eyes glued to the iPhone tracking screen, waiting for Staples vehicle to move.

'Yeah, says you, you said that hours ago.'

'Never mind the back chat, how's the egg coming on?'

Warren was in the need of a proper meal, a proper Sunday roast. For days he had existed on fried food and convenience meals.

'Here you go Sergeant.' Warren raised his eyebrows at the comment as Jimbo passed his eggs on toast.

'What did I tell you?' All good things come to those who wait, looks like we'll have to put the eggs on hold. Staples is on the move.'

Jimbo picked up the iPhone. 'Definitely on the move,' he mumbled through a mouthful of toast, as he watched the tracking dot flashing on the screen.

Warren was already on his feet, tucking the Sig into the back waistband of his trousers.

'When they do this on telly they never say how uncomfortable it is. Frying pan turned off?' Warren asked as he put on his jacket and picked up the car keys. 'Ready?

Jimbo on the other hand slapped the two eggs between the slices of toast and made a sarnie.

'Ready as I'll ever be,' Jimbo said, sarnie in hand as he put on his denim jacket.

The Fiesta was parked out of view around the back of the flat. Seatbelts fastened and ignition turned on, the engine purred.

Warren composed himself. 'Don't bloody lose him,' he said, as Jimbo signalled and moved away from the kerb. 'Which way?

Jimbo in the passenger seat had eyes on the iPhone screen. 'Looks like he's heading east through the town centre.'

'Right then, here we go.' He slipped the car into gear and moved away, turned left heading for the Clive Sullivan Way into the city.

With the aid of the tracker there was no fear of being caught out, they could tail Staples's BMW from a discreet distance. They watched the BMW travel through the town centre and onto Hedon Road.

'That's where we'll most likely end up,' Jimbo said as they passed HMP Hull heading towards the Holderness coast. Once past the prison it wasn't long before they could see the illuminated skyline above the petrochemical plant at Saltend.

'Where do you think he's heading?' asked Warren.

'Fucked if I know.' Jimbo had his eyes glued to the satnav. 'There's sod all out this way.' Staples was being careful, sticking to the speed limit. 'He's turning off towards Paull.' Paull was a small village on the River Humber, just outside the city. Its history dated back to the Domesday Book. The stagnating village had recently received good economic news, it had been selected to be the home of the new Siemens Wind Turbine manufacturing factory, but it was short lived, they backed out of the deal. 'Still moving,' he said, as they turned right, passing the petrochemical plant. 'He's in the village now. He's stopped, I reckon it could be the pub car park.'

Warren pulled into a secluded gateway on the edge of the village. 'Think we'd better go on foot. Be glad to stand up, the bloody Sig has worn a hole in my back.' They climbed out of the vehicle and Warren zipped up his jacket, which offered little protection from the Humber wind. 'You know the village?'

'Not real well, been a few times to the boozer. There's only one pub, the *Humber Tavern*, on the main street at the far end of the village. They do a good steak on a Thursday night.'

'I'll treat you to one when this is all over.'

'If we're still in one piece to enjoy it,' Jimbo had to add.

'Forever the pessimist aren't you?'

'You do have a plan?' asked Jimbo.

'Come on, what do you think?'

'Didn't think so.' He pulled the collar of his coat tight. 'Bloody cold.'

Both men were quiet with their own thoughts as they walked through the narrow main street. Warren thought it strange, Staples wasn't a native of the area, what the hell was he doing visiting 'sleepy hollow' on a dark winter evening? There was only one conclusion he could come up with.

Up to no good.

The village was quiet and dark with very few streetlights. Jimbo stopped them short of the pub.

'The car park is straight ahead next to the pub, the far end is open to a picnic area. But if we nip down here,' he pointed to an alleyway by the side of the *Humber Tavern*, 'we end up on the riverside path and come out with a bit of cover, close to the pub car park.'

The wind blew straight off the river and whistled down the alley, it was even stronger as they left the shelter of the high walls onto the river front. The sky was clear, offering a sparkling vista of Barton on the other side of the Humber. The navigation lights of a coaster passing down river made the scene look serene, *shame we can't enjoy the night*, Warren thought to himself as they made contact with the cinder path of the river front.

Slowly and as quietly as the cinder path allowed, they neared the parking area. A low brick wall ran along the front of the car park separating it from the path, so far so good, there were very few overhead lights. Crouching down they slowly made their way along the path, Warren raised his head above the wall and risked a look. The BMW was parked at the far end beneath the skeleton limbs of the poplar trees. Next to the BMW was parked a dark coloured 4x4, a Range Rover. Even in the dark Warren recognised it.

'Well that is a piece of luck,' Warren turned to face Jimbo, 'all our eggs in one basket, John, Bob *and* Staples.'

'Time to put that plan of yours into operation,' Jimbo said sarcastically in a low voice.

Warren looked at his young partner in crime and shook his head, then removed the Sig from his concealed holster, checked it, slid the breach and took a deep breath.

'Yeah, but this isn't quite what I was expecting.'

'What were you expecting?'

'No idea, but now I have a chance to take care of Staples, and maybe get Conway's rocks at the same time. You sure you're up for this? You can hang back, no probs.'

'Are *you* sure? I mean once you pull that trigger there's no going back…'

'If there was another way I'd take it,' he kept his eyes on the BMW as he spoke, not letting Jimbo see the trepidation in his face.

'Come on Ray you're not a killer…' Jimbo protested, not that he himself was afraid, which he was, but because it took a certain kind of person to kill another in cold blood and he wasn't sure if Warren was that kind of a person. 'Just think about it for a minute, it's not just Staples is it? There's three of 'em. And another thing have you actually fired that thing and I don't mean on some safe firing range?'

Warren was thinking on his feet.

'Now that *is* a question. Put it this way mate, there's always a first time for everything, right? Before you ask, yeah I'm nervous, but if I don't do this he will.' Warren swapped the Sig from hand to hand as he wiped his sweaty palms down his trousers.

'So what's the plan now?'

'We'll approach from the tree line, you keep behind me until Staples is taken care of.'

'Then?'

'If I don't get the answer I want, we do the unexpected.'

'And that is?'

'We take Bob hostage and hold him until John sees sense.'

'Fucking hell Ray, now we're going into kidnapping! Well I'm not having him in my bleedin' flat.'

Warren turned to face Jimbo. 'Has Conway a lock-up, somewhere we can take him?'

'He's got a few, but the small unit on the Dairycoates Industrial Estate sounds favourite, we use it for storing booze.'

'Why does it sound favourite?'

'Cos I've got the keys!'

'Nice, so here's the plan, I shove the Sig in John's face and give you the nod. You grab Bob, shove him in the boot of the BMW, we go back get the Fiesta and I follow you to the lock-up. You alright with this?' Jimbo nodded.

'Ok, let's go.' The lad was actually scared stiff. He'd done some serious things for Conway, but nothing as heavy as this.

Warren tucked the Sig back into his waistband, dropped down to his knees and began to 'commando' crawl beside the low brick wall.

'Ouch! For fuck's sake!' he heard Jimbo swearing under his breath as the sharp cinders of the path dug into the flesh of his hands.

Fifty metres further on, the path disappeared, creating a ditch-like hole, three feet deep. They were committed; there was no other approach. Warren eased himself over the edge where the path should have been and found himself knee deep in Humber mud. Jimbo continued his blaspheming as he joined Warren in the hole. Side by side they scrabbled up the opposite bank, wasn't as easy as the drop down had been.

Covered from head to toe in mud they lay side by side in the shadows, no words were spoken as they lay still until their breathing was back to normal. Once again composed, Warren looked to Jimbo and nodded, it was time. He eased himself to his knees and in a low crouched run he headed for the cover of the far tree line. He could hear Jimbo close behind.

Although the car park was devoid of lighting, thanks to a crescent moon they had a clear view of the Range Rover. John and Bob sat in the front seats, Staples was in the rear, leaning forward in the gap between the front seats. The conversation looked animated, with Staples pointing his index finger – a falling out amongst thieves? Warren reached around his back and removed the Sig, then reached into the breast pocket of his jacket and took out the suppressing silencer. Without a sound he attached it to the barrel of the weapon.

'You sure, Greg?' Jimbo whispered. He needed reassurance.

'I'm sure. You sure *you're* ready for this? I don't know what'll happen when I take Staples out, so if things go tits up and the shit hits the fan, don't hang about, just leg it.' He took the safety catch off the Sig.

Warren moved off low, with a firm two-handed grip on the Sig, his arms outstretched. Slowly and carefully he edged forward, Jimbo stayed in the security of the trees. Although he had the advantage of surprise on his side, Warren knew he couldn't take any chances with a man like Staples, he had to act swiftly and deadly. 'Shit,' he said under his breath as he heard something crunch loudly underfoot.

He risked a glance over his shoulder, Jimbo was still in the trees, waiting for the gun to fire, then he'd make his move, one way or another. The lad would have his use once Staples was taken care of, a plan was formulating as he stealthily approached.

So far so good, he'd reached the rear of the Range Rover without being seen surprisingly easily. The voices inside the vehicle seemed agitated; the occupants were deep in discussion. Warren stayed low at the rear of the vehicle, he knew what he was about to do was against all his principles; he also knew he had to carry it out regardless.

He readied himself. Remembering his training, he regulated his breathing, then unseen, slowly rose to his feet taking a wide led stance and with a two-handed grip aimed the Sig through the rear windscreen, and pulled the trigger. From such a close proximity the glass erupted into a million sharp shards as the bullet made contact. The silencer did its job, a quiet phut, followed by another – phut. Like the rear screen, the back of Staples head exploded on contact, the 9mm bullet passed straight through the skull, exiting through the forehead along with brain tissue and bone fragments. The second one hadn't been needed.

The jolt from the second bullet made Staples's body jar with shock and fall back into a reclining position on the back seat. Instinctively, John and Bob simultaneously ducked their heads down; they stayed down until they realised someone was opening the driver's side door. Slowly, they raised their heads to see Warren pointing the Sig at John's head. Their faces were masks of horror and shock, enhanced with blood and brain tissue.

As the first bullet smashed into the rear screen Jimbo was up on his feet and running, running to see what help he could be.

'Jimbo, get his car keys and check for a weapon.'

The lad was a bag of nerves as he opened the rear door of the Range Rover. The metallic smell of blood invaded his nostrils. He was tough, but even so his stomach heaved as he struggled to pull the dead weight of Staples's corpse towards him. He fumbled in Staples's trouser pockets for the BMW keys. He couldn't help but retch he reached inside the bloodied jacket and found the holstered weapon along with a silencing suppressor.

'Got it.'

'Take the safety off and get around the other side and watch my mate Bob,' Warren told him. The younger man took in a lungful of fresh night air. Jimbo wiped the bloody gunge from his hands on the car upholstery. He was in awe; he didn't think Warren had it in him to commit cold-blooded murder. He saw him in a new light – a dangerous one. He opened the nearside door, took a pace back and pointed the weapon at Bob's head. 'It would be wise not to make any sudden movements Bob, nothing worse than a nervous man with a gun,' Warren warned.

'Greg, to say we weren't expecting you would be an understatement, you obviously put two and two together,' John said as he wiped his face with the back of his hand. 'Bit of an extreme entrance don't you think?' John was hoping the show of bravado would unsettle Warren.

It didn't.

'Just put your hands on the steering wheel where I can keep an eye on them.' John placed his hand amongst the blood and brain tissue that had been sprayed over the dashboard and steering wheel. 'Don't take your eyes off Bob, Jimbo while I have a little chat with our friend here. First of all gentlemen, are you carrying any weapons?' Both men shook their heads. 'Then I'll trust you – but if I see your hands move an inch Jimbo will blow Bob's fucking brains all over you. Right Jimbo?' Bob's face visibly paled beneath the crimson splashes. Warren was sure, almost, that if it came to such a situation Jimbo wouldn't hesitate. 'One question, well two, why, and where are the diamonds?'

'What can I say Greg? Other than it was too good an opportunity not to take advantage of, it's not often one and half million pounds worth of untraceable diamond come within your reach.'

Bob just sat there not saying anything, hoping John could talk them out of the situation.

'Why me, why put the hit on me?' Warren's hands trembled, the Sig was getting heavy.

'We knew you would add up the numbers eventually, in all honesty we didn't expect the situation to escalate so quickly. Initially we just required you to gather information, but, well… things happen that we cannot always predict – don't they?'

'Well John, this is something else that you didn't predict. Ok Jimbo.' John, keeping his hands on the steering wheel turned his head and watched as Jimbo took a step forward and grabbed Bob by the collar of his jacket and heaved him from the vehicle. Bob tried to make his body a dead weight as he was dragged and forced to his knees.

Jimbo was getting into character, to his surprise his voice was steady, not showing any sign of nerves. 'Hands on your head, stand up slowly.'

Bob looked at John then across to Warren.

'I should do as he tells you Bob, remember what I said about a nervous man with a gun.'

'Now walk slowly to the back of the BMW.' Jimbo liked it, he prodded Bob hard in the centre of the back with Staples's 9mm Glock, at the same time pressing the remote locking on the BMW key fob with his free hand. The boot lid rose slowly. Unceremoniously, Jimbo pushed Bob forward. 'In you get.' Bob tried to turn to protest. 'Just fucking get in,' and Jimbo gave him a hand, by shoving him into the boot. Jimbo made a pretend motion of aiming the Glock and shooting, smiled and reached up to the boot lid and sent it down, catching Bob's head on the way.

Done. Feeling pleased with himself, Jimbo stood by the BMW, trembling.

'Now, John, very slowly with your left hand pass me your mobile – keep your other hand where it is.' John struggled, as he reached inside his right hand coat pocket for his mobile and passed it through the open window. 'The rest is very simple. I assume you want Bob back and I want the diamonds and the cash from the *Seabird*. Simple as that, oh yes and the class "A". One more thing, I want a written statement that I was in your employment, it clears me of any involvement in terrorism or any other crap you've tarnished me with. We meet in forty-eight hours and clear this misunderstanding up once and for all.' Warren keyed in the number of his pay-as-you-go into John's mobile and passed the phone back. 'You call me on this number. Because if you don't, Bob will end up the same way as Staples, and I swear I will find you and kill you. I've got nothing to lose, remember, you saw to that.'

'And you can add James Boland to that statement as well,' Jimbo said, proudly. Warren smiled at the lad's cheek.

'Surely we can discuss this…'

'No more discussions,' Warren said cutting him off. 'One more thing.' Warren opened the Range Rover door and lifted his right hand high and with the butt of the Sig he brought it down fast and hard, crunching the fingers of John's left hand against the steering wheel. John didn't make a sound as the pain shot up his hand and arm, it was excruciating. He had an act to keep up. 'Good job you drive an automatic. Twenty-four hours.'

Warren slammed shut the Range Rover door and walked over to where Jimbo was waiting. He didn't look back as he opened the driver's side door of the BMW, dropped into the seat and sighed heavily. 'Fuck,' he said as Jimbo sat beside him. 'Look at me,' he held out his arms, 'I'm shaking like a fucking leaf.'

'Well leave the shaking until we get out of here,' said Jimbo.'

'What about Staples?'

'Not our problem Jimbo, they have people to take care of that sort of thing. I'll drop you off at the motor and follow you back to the lock-up. Think we'd better ditch the Fiesta when we get back.'

'Shame I was just getting used to it.'

Chapter 32

The journey back through the city called for a careful but swift drive. Warren knew John would have already put out a report of a stolen BMW, of course he would omit to tell the authorities Bob was in the boot, it would be an 'identify, do not apprehend' report. Both vehicles kept to speed limits and made sure they obeyed the traffic signals, no jumping amber lights. Warren also kept one eye on the rear view mirror for flashing blue lights.

Conway's lock-up was a single-storey brick built unit at the bottom of a cul-de-sac on Dairycoates Industrial Estate down Hawthorne Avenue, close to Hessle Road. CCTV cameras covered every entrance and exit. Fortunately, Conway had made it his business to make sure that none of them worked. The same could be said of the on-site security team, a team of wankers who for the occasional back-hander turned a blind eye to his dealings. Warren could only praise Conway for his astuteness.

Jimbo stood by the car smoking a rollie. Warren pulled the BMW up close to the unit doors.

'Any bother?' asked Jimbo.

'No probs, no tails, nothing.'

'What about him in the boot?'

'The way you slammed the lid down he's probably dead.'

'Come on Greg, don't say things like that, I feel like a bag of crap as it is.'

'Greg? Did you call me Greg?' Warren reiterated surprised.

'Well that's your name init?'

'So we're pals again?' Warren laughed, this was what he'd been waiting for.

'Fuck off! Anyway, what's the next part of your master plan?'

'Well if he *is* dead…'

'I told you, don't make jokes like that!' He laughed, the tension was well and truly lifted.

'We get him inside out the way, make sure he's secure and have a word with him.' Jimbo raised his eyebrows. That night he'd seen Warren in different light. He didn't fancy being in Bob's shoes when Warren had 'a word' with him. 'Can you get rid of the motors and fix us up with another?'

'A bloke I know has a scrapyard just over the flyover, I'll give him a call to meet me there, he'll do owt for a few quid.'

Jimbo walked to the rollover door, unlocked the padlock and pushed up the door enough for them to get inside. Warren was surprised, it was like an alcoholic's paradise, knock-off imported beer, wine and spirits, cardboard cartons were piled high to the roof. 'Reckon we might get pissed when you come back. Got any tape?' Jimbo went through to the office and returned with two rolls of sticky tape. 'That will do nicely. Let's have him in.'

Much to Jimbo's pleasure, Bob was alive and almost kicking when the boot lid was popped, bleeding a little from a cut on the head – but still alive.

'Out, and don't try anything, Bobby,' Jimbo said, cockily, pointing his newly-claimed Glock at the man. Bob struggled, he could hardly move, he was battered and bruised from bouncing about in the confined space. 'Don't be such a tart,' said Jimbo, 'think yourself lucky it wasn't a Mini,' he told him as he eased his legs over the boot lip. Bob rocked on unsure legs that trembled as he put his full weight down. Jimbo was back into his new-found persona of 'gangsta' as he took a step back and gestured, waving with the Glock for Bob to enter the lock-up. He looked to Warren hoping for some kind of support, it didn't come.

'Don't look at me, just do as he tells you.' Jimbo paced up and down, waving his new toy.

'Well Bob, I never expected this situation to arise when I signed up – keep moving.' Bob limped his way through the cardboard cartons, 'Ok, that's far enough. Sit on the box.'

'What are you expecting to gain from abducting me, Greg?'

'Clear my name, get my job back, get the goods back, to be honest, I'm not sure that I care anymore.' He turned to Jimbo. 'Reckon I could get a job with Mick Conway, what do you reckon? Pass me the tape mate.' Warren commenced to tape their hostage's ankles together. 'Don't do anything silly Bob, just sit still. Hands down by your side.' Bob did as he was told. Warren bound his arms straight down to the side of his body, round and round with the parcel tape.

Jimbo grunted as he did what he'd seen Warren do, conceal the Glock in the rear waistband of his jeans. 'You're right,' he said wincing.

'Right about what?'

'It's bloody uncomfortable with a gun down your pants.'

Warren grinned. 'I think it would be wise if you didn't take it with you, there's a good chance they have the police looking for the Fiesta. Wouldn't look good for you to be picked up with a concealed weapon.'

'Good point,' he replied as he handed the Glock over. 'Right, I'll see you when I get back.'

'And you'd better get some bottles of water for our guest. Lock us in, need to get my head down for a few minutes.'

'It's alright for some,' he said, as he lifted the roller door just enough to duck under, then once outside he pulled the door back down and locked it.'

Warren heard the motor start and drive away.

'Now Bob, there's one way in and out – and it's locked, Jimbo has the only key. So just sit there like a good bloke.' Bob couldn't do anything even if he'd wanted to, trussed up like the proverbial Christmas turkey. 'We'll have our little chat later.'

Warren was shattered and wired at the same time, he was puzzled as to why he wasn't disturbed about earlier events.

His first kill.

The thing that bothered him was that he'd found it easy, too easy and he shouldn't have. He'd felt the same buzz when he'd shattered Billybob's leg. He looked around the lock-up; a case of *Glen's Finest Single Malt* caught his eye. He ripped the cardboard carton open, pulled out a bottle and held it high. 'Looks good Bob, fancy one?' He walked over to where Bob was trussed up, took the cap off the bottle and held the neck to Bob's lips.

Not being able to control the flow Bob spluttered, a little whisky running down his chin. 'Thanks.'

'No problem mate,' Warren said as he put down the bottle and picked up the roll of tape. 'Nothing personal,' he said as he wrapped the tape around Bob's head and mouth.

Once he was sure Bob couldn't pose a problem he sat down on the floor, lay his back against the cardboard and lifted the bottle high. 'Cheers,' he saluted and took a deep swallow, put the bottle on the floor beside him and closed his eyes.

He didn't even hear Jimbo coming back for the second vehicle. It was an hour later he was woken by the sound of the roller door being opened.

'Bloody hell, it's alright for some,' Jimbo headed straight for the bottle of whisky at Warren's side. 'Get anything out of him?' He inclined his head towards Bob as he brought the bottle to his lips.

'Couldn't be arsed, thought I'd let him stew a little.' Jimbo passed back the bottle. 'Get any water?'

Jimbo produced a plastic carrier bag. 'Got you a Big Mac as well.'

'Cheers pal, I'm starving, what about Bob here, got anything for him?'

'He can fucking wait till we get the gear back.'

'You're a hard man Jimbo, begrudging a man a burger.'

'Whatever. Fancy a brew?' Jimbo went through to the office and brewed up.

Jimbo lay on a crumpled heap of cardboard boxes and dozed, his mug still full beside him. It had been a long and eventful night. Warren had made short work of his burger and sat nursing a mug of strong instant coffee.

'Bob,' his head lifted, 'if I take the tape off are you going to behave?' Bob nodded agreement. 'Thought you might.' He put the mug on the floor, stood up and crossed over to Bob. 'You might want to grit your teeth,' he suggested as his hands found the edge of the tape and began to pull. Bob groaned loudly through the tape as it was pulled from around his head. 'Fucking hell Bob sorry about that,' he said as he held up the freed tape that now resembled a piece of coconut matting.

Bob's face was almost red raw where the adhesive had taken a good hold. 'I suppose I should thank you for that. Any chance of some of that water?' Warren picked up the plastic bottle and removed the cap then held the neck to Bob's lips. 'Thanks for that.' Water ran down his chin.

'I need to know a few things… what changed?'

'Needs, money, whatever – take your pick.'

Warren stood before Bob and drew back his fist.

Bob closed his eyes. 'No need for more violence Greg,' he said as he closed his eyes expecting the worst.

'You're right, you're not fucking worth it.' His arm dropped to his side.

'Ok, I'll tell you. As you know we needed someone on the inside of Conway's operation, someone who could garner information. Perhaps eventually creating themselves an opportunity to become indispensable. Then along came the diamonds. One point five million pounds worth of untraceable Blood Diamonds within our grasp, how often does an opportunity like that arise?'

'And Staples, why the hit on me?'

'It was never supposed to happen. Staples was to be long gone before you arrived on the scene. It was just unfortunate your paths crossed, one could say you were collateral damage.'

'I knew too much?'

'We knew you would do the maths and come up with the correct number, it was something we couldn't risk. You had to be removed.'

'You mercenary bastards,' said Warren.

'That may be so, the authorities were informed that Raymond Cole was not who he was alleged to be, he was a rogue police officer who had gone over to the dark side, with tenuous links to the Islamic State.'

'Because I'm black! That makes me a terrorist?'

'No, not on its own, but it helped. The photographs of you leaving a clandestine meeting in North London, with two prominent supporters of Isis went a long way in convincing the local police force.' Bob smiled and shrugged his shoulders. 'Subsequently, if you were not arrested you had to be eliminated and that's where Staples entered the equation. Staples had been with us for a number of years working both legitimately and on operations that were "off the books", I might add it proved to be lucrative for all parties. Staples had become a wealthy man. Unfortunately, he was coming to the end of his usefulness and if things should go awry as they did, he was expendable. And there you have it, do with it what you will.'

'Can I assume the police are still looking for me?'

'Of course, and your young colleague.'

'You're a pair of bastards – you know that?'

'It has been said. I don't suppose there is any chance you might take the rest of this tape off and make me a coffee?'

'You suppose correctly,' Warren said as he bound Bob's face none too gently with the parcel tape.

Chapter 33

'How much fucking longer do you reckon we'll be cooped up in here? I'm starving.' Jimbo was bored, they had been stuck in the lock-up all night and it was now mid-morning.

'Until we get the call from John, stop whinging and put the kettle on.' Warren's mobile signalled an incoming text message, he took out the mobile and checked the screen. It was from Grimes. *They know where you are, leave now*. 'Shit,' Warren said under his breath. He stood up and went through to the office where Jimbo was making yet another coffee. He passed over the mobile for Jimbo to read the message.

'How did they find out about this place?'

'They put two and two together or should I say three, you, Conway and me. This place would have already been known to the local intelligence, it will have been a process of simple elimination.

'So what now?'

'We get out of the place.'

'And him?' Jimbo nodded to Bob.

'He's our insurance, we'll have to take him with us. But we can hardly walk out the front door, we're probably already under surveillance. Any ideas?'

'As it happens, Conway had already plans in place in case anything like this should come up.'

Warren was warming to Conway. His opinion of Conway was still one of a fat arrogant fucker, but one who knew the score and planned for it.

'Well, I don't think you should keep it to yourself, we don't know how long we've got until an armed response team turns up hammering on the door.'

Warren followed Jimbo back into the main unit. 'Give us a hand with these,' he started to shift boxes away from the back wall. 'Come on, cop a hold, careful. Mind you, don't drop 'em, but I don't suppose it'll matter, the coppers will fill their boots with the stuff.' He started to shift boxes and cartons away from the back corner. Both men were breathing heavy and caked with sweat, finally the exterior wall was clear. Jimbo looked to Warren and smiled, put both hands into readymade crevices, pulled and a full section of the interior skin came away.

'Where does it lead to?'

'The unit that backs onto us.'

'Who's it belong to?'

'Fucked if I know, stop asking so many questions.' *Cheeky sod* thought Warren. 'The motors at the end of the block, I'll go fetch it while you grab your mate and we can be away. Then they can hammer away on the door till they get fucking fed up.'

It didn't seem right, Jimbo taking command of the situation, but Warren didn't argue, just did as he was told.

'Time to leave, Bob.' He could hear Jimbo pulling at the chains of the roller door in the adjacent unit. Warren removed the tape from around his legs and grabbed him roughly from his perch on the boxes. Bob's legs had cramped up and he struggled to keep his balance.

'Got to help me out a bit here Bob, or I'll just drag you by your feet,' Warren told him as he tried to manoeuvre him between the boxes towards the hole in the wall. Bob's legs were cramped, he could hardly move them. 'Sorry Bob, but if you won't help…' he said, as he put a hand on Bob's head and pushed him forward and through into the next unit.

Jimbo was as good as his word, two minutes later Warren heard a motor pull up. He left the engine running and came to Warren's assistance. Bob was manhandled through the partially opened door. 'Sorry about that,' Warren said as Bob's head clanged against the metal of the roller door. 'This all you could get?'

Jimbo had found them an ancient rust and white Transit van.

'Come on Greg, it was short notice, beggars can't be choosers, it's the only thing he had that would start.' He opened the side sliding door. 'Come on Bobby, shift yourself.' Bob groaned, collecting even more bruises as he was manhandled into the back of the van and the door slammed shut.

'Where to?' Jimbo asked, as they took their seats in the front.

'Don't know yet, just drive, let's get the hell away from here and what the hell is that smell?!'

'Before it was sent for scrap it was used for wet-fish deliveries,' Jimbo said with all seriousness, as he drove the non-descript van out through the industrial estate's one-way system.

Simultaneously, 200 metres down the road a convoy of police vehicles drove through the entrance of the estate.

'Just in the nick of time,' he said as he turned the van left down Hawthorn Avenue, towards Anlaby Road.

'There is one place we could check out.'

'And where's that?'

'Home. I'd almost forgotten about the place, seems a lifetime since I was last there.'

For almost half an hour they cruised up and down Delapole Avenue, checking Warren's three-bedroomed, semi-detached house wasn't under surveillance.

'Pull up here Jimbo, I'll take a walk around the back and make sure it's all clear.' Jimbo pulled the Transit into the kerb side some 200 metres from the house. Warren opened the door and dropped down to the pavement and swiftly disappeared down a ten-foot access alley between the houses that led around the back.

Jimbo cruised on.

Warren was sure that any surveillance that was on the place would have been withdrawn long ago. All things being equal, he hoped they were now employing their thin resources in other areas. Nevertheless, he took it slowly and carefully all the while trying not to look suspicious, which was not easy for a dirty looking six foot two bloke, in need of a bath and change of clothes.

Satisfied the coast was clear he scaled his own back fence, the tall timber door being bolted on the inside. Warren scrambled over the top and dropped down. *Sanctuary*, he hoped. Fortunately, against his initial instructions he'd kept a set of house keys with him, just in case. He put the key in the back door, unlocked it and stepped inside. He sighed; it felt good to be on familiar territory. A quick scrutiny confirmed his initial thoughts, the place had already been searched – professionally. Things were hardly out of place, just one or two giveaway tales. He closed the curtains as he went through the house. Satisfied, he called Jimbo on the mobile with instructions, then went out back and unlocked the double garden gates. Two or three minutes later he heard the rough engine of the Transit coming down the ten-foot, he opened the gates and Jimbo backed the rusty heap into the back garden parking area.

He opened the nearside door. 'Give us a hand to get him inside.' Warren slid open the sliding door, the stink of rotten fish seemed even worse. Bob was a mess, trussed up he had no control of his body and he'd rolled back and forth amongst the filth in the back of the van. Unceremoniously, Warren grabbed him by the shoulders and heaved him out of the van, causing more bruising that would likely bother him later. Jimbo shut the Transit doors.

'On your feet Bobby, hope you can walk because I'm too tired to carry you.' Between them they helped Bob stand upright and steadied him as they made their way along the path to the back door. Once inside, Warren pulled out a kitchen chair. 'Park yourself on there,' he said, as he forced Bob to sit.

The second thing Warren did was to switch on the boiler, he was looking forward to a refreshing hot shower.

'Very nice,' said Jimbo as he walked through the back door, and looked around the tidy kitchen. 'Beats slumming it at my place.' Tired, he pulled out a chair, sat next to Bob and pulled a grimacing face. 'For a posh bloke you don't half stink!'

'You hungry?' Warren asked as he searched the freezer, 'there's not much – fancy pizza?'

'Sounds good to me, how about you Bobby?' Jimbo asked the mummified hostage, who was now in such a state he could barely nod his head without pain.

'Better get the oven on then.'

Chapter 34

'Well this is almost civilised,' Bob said as the three men sat around the kitchen table. The tape had been removed from around his head and mouth, also his left arm had been freed to allow him to feed himself. After all Warren *was* civilised. The three men ate pizza hungrily and washed it down with a bottle or two of beer.

'Keep your eye on him Jimbo, while I have a quick shower.' Warren left them still sitting around the table.

'So Bobby, was you a copper before you became a spook?' asked Jimbo

'Military Intelligence and will you please stop calling me Bobby.'

'You mean you were in the SAS?'

'Goodness grief no, far too dangerous, I was a desk jockey evaluating intelligence reports and sending others to carry out the dangerous stuff.'

'What about your oppo, whatcha call him… John, what did he do?'

'Ahh well, you'll have to ask him that yourself when you meet him. If you're still alive when that happens.'

'Thanks for that thought mate. Give me your arm.' He pulled Bob to his feet and helped him shuffle through to the living room. He dropped Bob down on the sofa. 'Might as well get comfortable.' He put the Glock on the dining table on the opposite side of the room and dropped down on the sofa next to Bob.

Warren was glad of the reprieve, a few minutes alone. He set the shower going and stripped off the clothes he'd been wearing for goodness knows how many days and dropped them in the washing basket. He opened the shower cubicle door and stepped into the steam. Standing under the hot spray he let the power shower do its stuff, his muscles eased as the hot water ran down his aching body. As he towelled himself dry he began to feel more like his old self, with his towel wrapped around his waist he padded barefoot to the bedroom and rummaged through his belongings for clean clothes.

All was quiet downstairs, something he was going to take advantage of. He lay on top of his bed and was asleep minutes after his head touched the pillow.

But not for long.

Chapter 35

Warren woke with a start, possibly some built-in survival instinct, he sat up straight and rubbed his eyes with his knuckles. He swung his legs to the floor and walked over to the window, then gently teased the edge of the curtain free and looked out into the darkness – nothing. He'd had a similar feeling the night he'd been followed by the hillbilly, *paranoia*, he thought and shrugged it off. Another quick glance into the night and then he went downstairs to be greeted by the sound of both men snoring. He couldn't help but laugh to himself at the sight of the two men who sat side by side on the sofa, Bob trussed up with parcel tape and Jimbo with his head resting on Bob's shoulder – a strange display.

Warren went through to the kitchen and made three mugs of instant coffee before waking the sleeping pair. He ripped free the tape from Bob's face. Bob yelped with shock and both men sat up straight immediately, Jimbo embarrassed. 'Easy boy,' said Bob 'you can rest your head anytime.'

Warren was surprised how Bob had it in him to joke given his situation.

'Fuck off, I was just resting my eyes and my head dropped that's all,' Jimbo protested.

Warren freed Bob's left arm and passed over the steaming mug.

'Now you've had a chance to think about things I'm going to ask a question, and if you really don't want to end up like Staples I advise you to answer truthfully. Where are the diamonds?'

'In a safe location.'

'Do you have access to them?'

'Ah, well…'

'No not "ah well", I think it's about time we stopped this fucking about.' He reached across and took the mug out of Bob's hand. 'If you know where they are I think you'd better tell me.' He walked over to the dining table and picked up Jimbo's newly-acquired Glock and attached the silencer.

Bob was visibly sweating. 'Greg I really don't think there's any need for violence…'

'Just answer the question Bob, do you know where the diamonds are?'

This was the second time since the assault on Staples that Bob looked really worried, his eyes fixed on the Glock. Once upon a time he would have sworn Warren wouldn't use the weapon – now he wasn't so sure. 'You really should be having this conversation with John.'

'Enough, I need a straight answer.' Warren picked up the parcel tape and stuck a length over Bob's mouth. Bob mumbled something unintelligible beneath the tape. He went back to the dining table and dragged a chair across the room and placed it directly in front of Bob. 'I was hoping it wouldn't come to this,' he said as he sat down, 'time to stop pissing about.' Warren was sat so close to Bob he could smell the rotting fish radiating from his clothes. He took the safety catch off the Glock, pulled back the breach and pushed the barrel into Bob's groin. Bob's forehead glistened with sweat at the prospect of having his balls blown off. He was still mumbling. Fear set in the hostage's eyes.

'Greg, think about what you're doing, you've already killed one man, you don't want another death on your conscience.' Warren looked Bob in the eye and withdrew the gun.

Bob sighed with relief beneath the tape. Then he pointed the Sig towards the floor and pulled the trigger. *Phut – v*ery quietly but messily a 9mm bullet tore through Bob's once highly polished shoe and his right foot. Compared to taking out Staples this was easy, after all Bob still had another leg – for now.

Jimbo sat there not believing what had just happened, like Bob, he thought it was just a threat, a frightener. He couldn't believe it when the trigger was pulled and Bob in a reflex action fell forward off the sofa groaning in agony beneath the tape. 'Greg, for fuck's sake what are you doing mate?'

'We want the goods back don't we?' he snapped, reaching forward and ripping the tape from covering Bob's mouth. 'Well – talk or you'll have a hole in the other foot,' he said as he ripped the tape from Bob's mouth.

He gasped and sobbed. 'There was no need… I've had enough and was always going to tell you,' he stuttered between breaths, 'they're in the office safe… they were there when you did your breaking and entering…'

Jimbo jumped to his feet. 'Typical, fucking typical, why didn't *you* think of that?'

Warren ignored him. Even if he'd wanted to, there would have been no way he would have been able to open the safe without the code and key.

'So – we have to go back and do it again, only this time we can go in the front door. Can't we Bob?'

Bob nodded, he was pale and going into shock.

'Don't you reckon we should get him to hospital?'

'It's like the burger Jimbo, once we've got everything back, he can have a burger while they're repairing his foot.'

Warren went through to the kitchen and came back with a couple of tea towels.

'Patch him up best you can so he doesn't bleed to death in the meantime.' Warren went through all of Bob's pockets. He found his keys, including those that he hoped would open Gemmell Strategies. 'Bob, you still hear me?' Bob opened his eyes and blinked through the pain and gave a contemptuous look. 'Is there a code for the safe?' He shook his head. 'You are telling me the truth?' Warren pressed the barrel of the Glock into the top of his left shoe. Again Bob nodded, this time more vigorously. Warren went into the kitchen and returned with a pad of paper and a pen. 'Write down the front door code,' he gestured with the Glock. Bob didn't need asking twice and wrote down the access code.

Jimbo came over with the sticky tape and stuck a length over Bob's face. Then nodded towards the kitchen. Warren followed.

'What's on your mind?' Warren asked.

'Him, what the fuck we gonna do with him? We can hardly take him with us when we go back?'

'To be honest with you Jimbo, I don't give a toss if he croaks it.'

'Well he's hardly gonna do that is he? He's only got a fuckin' hole in his foot.'

The conversation didn't get any further, Warren's mobile vibrated in his pocket. He checked the screen – it was DI Grimes.

'Thanks for the tip off by the way,' Warren said on answering.

'Glad to be of help. I take it you're somewhere safe?'

'For the time being.' Warren was pleased to hear a friendly voice.

'I heard you've had a bit of bother?'

'You could say that. With a little luck this could soon be over.'

'Well you know where I am if you need anything, if I hear anything I'll be in contact.'

'Cheers Bill, I appreciate the help.'

He hung up.

'Who was that?'

'The bloke who tipped us off back at the lock-up.'

'Have you got another one of your brilliant plans?' Jimbo asked, sarcastically.

'Maybe, but I think we ought to try and do something to keep Bob from bleeding all over my carpet. There's a first aid box in the top right hand side kitchen cupboard.'

Jimbo went through to the kitchen and Warren kneeled on the floor in front of Bob. 'I could say I was sorry but I'd be lying,' he said, 'the two of you have been playing me for a fool and well – enough was enough,' he said, as he carefully eased off Bob's shoe and sock.

'Hell Greg, take it easy,' Bob said between clenched teeth.

'Stop being such a wimp.'

'If you hadn't shot me in the first place… shit,' his foot throbbed in agony. 'I thought you were being careful?'

'You didn't give me any other alternative, just shut up and let me see what I can do.'

Jimbo came back with the first aid kit and placed it on the floor beside Warren.

Warren checked the contents. 'Afraid there's not much in here for gunshot wounds.'

'I would have been surprised if there had been.' Bob was trying hard to keep it together, he wasn't a brave man.

Warren set about cleaning the wound with an antiseptic wipe. 'I think you'll live,' he said as he placed a pad of soft gauze over and beneath the wound and bound it tight with a crepe bandage.

'So what's the latest plan?' asked Jimbo.

'I've just said, we go back.'

'And?' he walked towards the kitchen and inclined his head towards Bob.

'If we don't take him with us, how do we know he isn't taking the piss and giving us the wrong code? If that's his idea we may as well hand ourselves in now. On the other hand, if we take him with us and he *is* stringing us along, he saw what happened to Staples and knows the consequences.'

'Jesus, Greg, I'm not sure anymore.'

'Look mate, if you want to bail out that's fine, but with or without you I have to go back.'

'Fuck – well I'm not going to carry him.' Jimbo opened the fridge took out a bottle of beer. 'When are we doing this?'

'Tonight, I want this over with.'

They went back through to the lounge, where Bob lay groaning on the sofa. 'Come on Bobby, give it a rest, you've only got a hole in your foot.'

Bob glared. If he'd been capable he would have jumped up and wrung Jimbo's neck.

'Ok matey I reckon you can take some of that tape off, I don't think he will be going anywhere.'

Jimbo freed Bob from his bonds.

'These might help,' said Warren as he gave Bob a glass of water and a couple of painkillers.

'And they're going to do a lot of good,' Bob said sarcastically through gritted his teeth as Jimbo helped him into the sitting position.

'Bob, got a proposition for you,' said Warren.

'One that doesn't involve me doing a spot of line dancing I hope?' trying to do his best at humour in the crap situation he found himself.

'Maybe, when your foot's healed. Seriously, I want you to come with us when we go back to the office.'

'Do I have a choice?'

'Not if you want medical attention, on the other hand gangrene will have set in before anyone finds you.'

'Well seeing as though you put it like that, how can I refuse? I will be delighted to accompany you.' He said through a grimace. The pain was now intense – he didn't know how he would get through. It wouldn't be long before shock set in.

'Jimbo, get Bob a Scotch, make it a large one.'

'Thought we needed one as well,' said Jimbo as he passed out the glasses.

Chapter 36

A crappy Transit van with three men sitting in the front, driving into Gemmell Strategies car park in the dark of night, couldn't have looked anything but suspicious on the site security camera.

'We'll have to move pretty quick Greg, it'll only be a matter of minutes before security come to check things over.'

'How quick we are depends on you, Bob.'

Jimbo opened the nearside door and jumped down to the floor, Warren, leaving the keys in the ignition climbed out and walked around the nearside and between them they helped Bob out and to the entrance porch. Warren unlocked the door and immediately the alarm box flashed and gave out a high pitched whine.

'Don't worry,' Bob said as he hobbled over to the box and punched in the code. 'The safe's in the office – upstairs.'

'Might have bleedin' known,' grumbled Jimbo at the thought of having to get Bob up a flight of stairs.

With Bob sandwiched between them they struggled, pausing every couple of steps. It was only one level up but they were panting and puffing by the time they reached Bob's office.

'Thank fuck there's only one floor,' said Jimbo as they manhandled Bob into the office.

'Key.' Warren held out his hand as Bob dropped down into his own chair.

'Safe's in the floor behind John's desk,' he said as he passed it over, then sat back in the chair with his hands on his knees under the desk.

'Keep an eye on him, Jimbo.' Warren dropped to his knees behind John's desk, pulled back a rug covering the safe, put the key in the lock and turned. He was half expecting an alarm to go off as he pulled the door open. 'So Bob, you *can* tell the truth,' he said from behind the desk.

'In the state I'm in there wouldn't be much point in lying.' Bob lay back with his eyes closed, the pain showing in his face.

Inside were the diamonds, the drugs and the cash plus an unexpected bonus, an extra ten thousand pounds in crisp fifty pound notes.

'Is it all there? asked Jimbo.

'And a bit more,' said Warren. 'Pass me the bag.'

Jimbo took off the rucksack he'd brought and passed it over.

Warren filled the bag. 'Time to go.'

Taking an arm each they helped or more like trundled Bob down the stairs. The alarm was reset, and they left locking the door behind them. The entire escapade had taken them less than ten minutes.

'Does it register with the security office when the alarm is deactivated?' Warren asked Bob.

'Unfortunately, yes.' Bob was sweating, the pain was getting worse.

'So we can assume John will know someone's accessed the office.'

'Normally security wouldn't bother, but with what's been going on we have to assume the worst.'

Once again luck was with them, the security van was driving into the estate as they left.

Chapter 37

They drove out of the business park and onto the Clive Sullivan Way, heading towards the city. The Transit definitely wasn't built for comfort; Bob felt every jolt and bump as they bounced them along on shock absorbers that barely did the job. After a couple of miles Warren turned off into the McDonald's parking area, pulled up and switched off the engine.

'I need a piss,' said Jimbo opening the door and dropping down to the floor.

'Bring some coffees back with you,' Warren called after him as he fished in his pocket for his mobile. 'Just going to send a text.' He was contacting John. 'Sent, just have to wait,' he said placing the mobile behind the steering wheel on the dashboard. 'Look Bob, I never meant for this to happen, well, I mean, putting a hole in your foot was power for the cause, right?'

'You may well look at it that way, it's more a matter of opinion,' Bob answered.

The mobile vibrated on the dash, he picked it up and checked the display. It was John. Warren opened the cab door and dropped down. 'About time,' he said into the mobile as he walked around the back of the van. John tried to take the advantage by setting the location for the meeting. 'No,' said Warren, 'we meet on my terms,' he gave him the location. 'And be alone, no surprises.' He hung up.

'Things look like they might be coming to an end and the three of us are still alive aren't we, that's got to be a bonus?' Warren said when he climbed back into the Transit.

'So far, Greg, as long as you keep that gun in its holster, I can live with a hole in my foot and about that…'

'I can't take you to the infirmary, you know that. Not with a gunshot wound? You know the protocol, the medics will be onto the police in a shot, no pun intended. On top of that, how do I know I can trust you not to turn us in yourself?'

'Have you heard yourself? When we were at the office I had my hand on the panic button. If I'd pressed it you would have been no wiser until an Armed Response Unit blew your head off. BUT I NEVER. You can trust me. Give me a pad and paper.' Warren fished about in the glove box and found an old petrol receipt and biro and handed it over. 'When you leave for the meet, call this number and tell them where to pick me up, there'll be no questions asked, just say an officer requires medical attention and give them the location. Don't worry I'll keep quiet. I want to keep my job, I can worry about my pension fund another day.' It was clear as the minutes went by Bob that was getting worse, Warren knew he needed medical attention as soon as possible.

Jimbo came back with a tray of cardboard cups of coffee and handed them out. 'Heard from Bobby's mate yet?'

Warren looked at the dashboard clock. 'Yep, it's on for tonight. In about an hour but I want to be there early, so we'll go as soon as we've finished the coffee.'

Bob sat between them, occasionally wincing with the pain. He popped another couple of paracetamol and washed them down with the coffee. It was obvious over the counter painkillers didn't do much good for a gunshot wound. Warren and Jimbo sat quiet, each with their own thoughts.

'Ok Bob, it's time for us to go, I have your word you won't try to contact John?'

'You have my word Greg. John and I are partners in a business sense only, he would do the same if it meant saving his own skin. Just get me to a doctor.'

'Jimbo give me hand getting Bob out. Going to sit you over there ok?' Bob just winced an acknowledgement. Carefully they assisted Bob from the van and they helped him over to a slatted bench outside of the restaurant. 'I'll make the call in ten minutes,' he told Bob.

'Take it easy Bobby,' Jimbo said as they got back in the van. They drove away leaving Bob close to passing out.

Chapter 38

Back on the Clive Sullivan Way they headed into the town centre.

'Now will you tell me where we're going?'

'Pryme Street, the multi-storey car park. We're – I'm meeting John on the top deck in the open. Once I get the letter we're out of there.'

The rush hour was just about over and the traffic was reasonably light through the town centre one-way system. Warren drove along Ferensway, past the new Transport Interchange and turned down by what used to be the Circus-Circus Bar, left past the Farm Foods store and then right into Pryme Street. Once inside the car park forecourt he stopped the van.

'So far so good Jimbo, drive up to the top deck and park up out of the way, but make sure you have a good view in case we have to make a quick exit. I'm going to take a look around. First I've got to make that call, get Bob some help.'

He took the Sig from the shoulder holster, checked the weapon and released the safety catch and re-holstered the weapon then climbed out of the van. Warren took out his mobile and dialled the number Bob had given him. The call was answered almost immediately. 'An officer needs urgent medical attention for a gunshot wound, McDonald's on St Andrews Quay, Hull.' He hung up before there was any chance of a being trace being made. Slowly and carefully he checked each level of the multi-storey, he didn't put it past John to have an armed response team lurking in the shadows.

On each level he wove between the parked vehicles checking the shadows. He reached the top deck without finding anything suspicious. Plenty of vehicle still remained parked giving him ample cover. The Transit was visible parked up between and Ford and a Citroen, he saw Jimbo slink low behind the steering wheel.

Warren made his way to the maintenance shed in the centre of the top floor parking area. He checked his watch, five minutes to go, he got out of sight and waited. A black four-wheel drive appeared. John was on time and he looked to be alone. The 4x4 came to a stop, John leaned forward over the steering wheel checking for anything untoward. Warren walked into the open and showed himself, arms outstretched showing he was unarmed. John flashed the vehicle lights and slowly edged forward. Two car lengths from Warren he stopped, switched off the ignition and climbed out.

'Where's your young colleague?' he called over.

'Just you and me John, just you and me.' Warren was tempted to take the Sig from its holster but didn't want to provoke the situation – yet.

'Have you brought my disclaimer?'

'I have indeed, right here in my pocket,' he patted the left breast pocket of his suit jacket. 'But first I believe you have something that belongs to me?'

'You give me the statement and I give you Bob. That was the deal.'

'Ahh but that was before you felt that you had to steal the diamonds, why?'

'Not steal John – reclaim. You'd never have given them up, let's face it the trust is no longer there, John.'

Warren walked closer, holding out his left hand. 'The statement?'

'You have the diamonds with you?' John asked as he reached into his inside pocket for the statement.

'I have. Stop – use your left hand, slowly.' He didn't want John's hand suddenly appearing holding an automatic weapon. 'But like I said, they were part of the original deal.'

John reached awkwardly reached into the jacket pocket. He withdrew his hand and brown envelope.

'Before I hand this over I also need assurances, assurance that our extra-curricular activities won't be revealed.'

'You have my word, I'll keep my mouth shut, you've no worries on that score.'

'Why don't I believe you Greg?'

'It's just your devious nature getting the best of you. You're not used to dealing with honest people.'

John laughed. 'When you've been in this game as long as I have you believe no one, not even yourself.'

'You've never asked about Bob?'

'Yes, how is Bob? Still alive?' He sounded as if he couldn't care less one way or the other.

'Still alive, hand over the statement and I'll tell you where to find him.' He wasn't about to say Bob was probably receiving treatment as they spoke.

John took two steps forward, the statement in his hand. Swiftly, with the skill of a professional, his right hand reached around his back. The next thing Warren knew he was facing the barrel of a 9mm Glock. Warren took a half a step forward in a futile attempt to disarm him.

'Easy, Greg, take out your weapon and lay it on the floor in front of you, carefully.'

Warren didn't have much of an option, he knew John would use the weapon – was going to use it.

Then the unexpected happened, he heard the rough sound of the Transit's engine. Bob turned – too late, the front of the van knocked John to the floor, he dropped the gun and the letter as the bumper smashed into his legs and continued going forward.

The engine was turned off and Jimbo climbed out to see his handiwork. 'Jesus, the brakes are knackered, I only meant to give him a nudge. Is he dead?' Jimbo asked as he went down on one knee and retrieved the Glock.

Warren dropped to his knees next to Jimbo. John's lower body was hidden underneath the Transit. He looked unconscious – or dead. He put two fingers to John's neck and felt for a pulse. 'He's a lucky bastard, still breathing. Thanks for that by the way, another couple of minutes and I'm sure he would have used the Glock.' He picked up his own weapon and the envelope from the floor, opened it and quickly scanned through the document. He was surprised; it actually did clear them both, stating they were operating lawfully on the instruction of Gemmell Strategies. 'Right, pal, we're in the clear. See if you can reverse that heap off him without causing any further damage.'

'Why don't we just take the 4x4?'

'I think we've had enough problems with GPS trackers don't you? Right, get it off him.'

Jimbo climbed back in the cab of the Transit, started the engine, the shift gear crunched into reverse and then the van very slowly reversed, revealing John and his mangled legs. Warren climbed into the passenger seat, took out his mobile and made an

anonymous call to the Emergency Services. *It was becoming a habit.*
'Ok, matey, time to get out of here.'

Chapter 39

'Are you sure about this?' asked Jimbo.

'Mate, you're such a worrier,' Warren replied as he looked over his shoulder for anything untoward.

'Yeah but I know your plans, they don't always work out.'

'Cheeky bugger, get on with it.'

'I don't like this one little bit Greg. Mick will go ballistic when he finds us in here.'

'Yeah well, maybe – just get the lock open.'

Jimbo concentrated and with practised fingers he manipulated the lock-pick. It was a simple job for someone with his skills to open the back door of Mick Conway's house.

'Ok we're in,' he said, relieved. 'I'd have thought Mick would have had something a bit more sophisticated than this,' he said as he opened the door, not sure if the alarm would be set or not – it wasn't.

'Good man, let's get into the warm and go find a drink while we wait.'

Warren thought this was one of his better plans, an unannounced visit. Although Jimbo was right, Conway wouldn't be very happy at having his home broken into, especially by the man whose legs he wanted to break. The house was in darkness but posed no problems, Jimbo knew it as well as he did his own small flat. They made their way into the living room and helped themselves to Conway's best malt whisky. Then with a glass of Conway's single malt they sat in the darkness of the living room and waited.

Two glasses of whisky later they heard the front door being opened. 'Stay cool Jimbo, let me do the talking,' Warren said in a low voice. A minute later Conway walked into the living room and flicked the light switch.

'What the fuck…' Warren smiled. Conway on the other hand looked as if he was about to have coronary. 'How the fuck did you two get in here?' he demanded.

'Through the back door? No damage done. I tell you what Mick, you should really upgrade your security and remember to switch on the alarm, any undesirable could have got in here. Now why don't you just get yourself a drink?'

Conway walked further into the room. 'I can see you two have drunk half the bottle already. You know how much that cost? He pointed to their glasses. 'Forty-five fucking quid a bottle that's how much, and you're knocking it back like it's Asda's own.'

'Don't be such a tight arse, I – we've got a proposition to put to you.'

Conway looked towards Jimbo, daring him to speak so he could shoot him down.

'Proposition? What can you fucking offer me?'

Warren reached into his pocket and pulled out the envelope containing the cash and tossed it over.

'What's this?'

'That Mick – is the twelve thousand pound you were going to buy the "H" with from the Dutchmen. Minus some expense money of course.' Conway ripped open the package. 'I think you'll find there's ten grand, give or take.'

'What's the catch?'

'No catch Mick, I said we'd get your money back, didn't I?' Conway visibly mellowed. He picked up the bottle of Scotch, poured himself a large one and offered the bottle over. 'Don't mind if we do.'

Conway had already picked up on the strange partnership between the tough black man and the young scally.

Jimbo was next with a surprise for Conway.

'We thought you might be able to make use of this Mick.' He stood up and walked over and handed over a taped up Tesco carrier bag, then returned to his seat.

Conway took the offered 'gift' and ripped off the tape to reveal another sealed up parcel.

'Well I fucking never – it's almost like Christmas. This the "H" from the *Seabird*?' Jimbo nodded and smiled. 'You going to tell me what the fuck's going on here?'

'You've heard that saying, "if I tell you that I'll have to kill you"?' Warren half joked.

'You mean that don't you?' His face suddenly sullen.

'Mick, let's just say there's a lot of stuff gone down over the past weeks and you really don't want or need to know about it. Honest.'

'How much do you want?' he asked, suspiciously.

'Nothing, it's a gift from me and Jimbo.'

'You think I'm fucking daft?' He knocked back his drink and refilled his glass. 'What's the catch?'

'Like I said, no catch. I'd say this makes us quits, wouldn't you? You got your cash back and a nice bonus that puts you well into profit.'

'What about the diamonds?'

'Ahh, now that's different. If we're honest about this, the diamonds were never *actually* yours to start with.'

'Yeah but Big Jim and the Dutch dealer…'

'As far as they're concerned the *Seabird* was turned over and the couriers killed, which is true. As I see it they have no reason to know any different. What do you reckon?'

'You have the diamonds?'

'Maybe – maybe not, it all depends.'

'Keep talking.' He was interested again.

'How much do you reckon they'd fetch on the open market?'

'In the raw state, uncut, they're worth somewhere in the region of eighty grand, maybe one fifty when they're cut and polished.'

'That right? Tut, tut, tut, what would you say if I told you I'd had them valued? Quite frankly I reckon you're taking the piss.' Warren picked up his drink, sipped then carefully put down the cut-glass tumbler and stood up. 'You ready for the off, Jimbo?'

Jimbo finished his drink and stood up ready to leave. It was a stalemate as both parties waited for the other to call their bluff.

Conway folded.

'Hang on a minute, surely we can talk about this?'

'Ball's in your court Mick, you start talking real money or we're leaving.'

'Ok, ok, you're right, when they're dressed a fair estimate would be somewhere in the region of one point five million, ok?'

'Sounds more like it,' the two men returned to their seats. 'This is what I had in mind, we do a split, fifty – fifty,' Warren knew this was pushing things a bit.

'Steady Ray.' The 'Ray' made Jimbo smile, he looked to Warren but kept his mouth shut. 'I see things a bit differently, I'm the one who will have to sit on them for fuck knows how long until all the fuss dies down and who knows when that'll be? So, I'm thinking two hundred grand, how does that grab you?'

This was what Warren had been expecting all along, selling the diamonds was a thing he couldn't do himself, Conway was the one with the contacts.

'It's a pittance Mick, we might as well piss off now.'

'Two fifty, final offer.'

'You drive a hard bargain Mick,' he held out his hand to shake, 'how soon can you have the cash?'

'How soon can you let me have the diamonds,' he countered.

'Now.' Conway was surprised, he stood up and walked out of the room and up the stairs, they could hear him above them.

'Safe's in his bedroom,' said Jimbo.

Warren smiled. 'Looking good Jimbo,' he said and poured himself another glass of Conway's expensive whisky. It wasn't long before Conway returned carrying an expensive looking briefcase. He walked across the living room and placed the case on the table.

'Show me,' he said to Warren as he sat down.

Warren stayed where he was and put his hand in his trouser pocket and pulled out a small drawstring bag and tossed it across the room. The fat man almost fell off his chair as he reached out to catch the bag. With his fingers trembling in anticipation, Conway loosened the drawstring and tipped the diamonds on to the table.

'They all there?'

'Each and every one.'

Conway touched each stone with care and then one by one he replaced them in the pouch and smiled, he'd secured himself a good deal. He flicked the catches on the briefcase, the lid opened to reveal its contents, two hundred and fifty thousand pounds in used notes of various denominations. 'It's all there – you can keep the case.'

Warren stood and walked over to examine the contents; Jimbo stood looking over his shoulder as he picked up the bundles and flicked through, then closed the lid.

'I'll take your word it's all there, Mick, it's been a pleasure doing business with you.' He patted the case with the palm of his hand.

He picked up the whisky bottle and refilled their glasses. 'To us,' he toasted.

'To us,' Conway and Jimbo said in unison.

Warren put down the glass and picked up the briefcase. 'I'll be in touch.'

'Do me a favour Ray, don't fucking bother,' said Conway, earnestly.

'You coming Jimbo?'

'So you've got yourself a new employer have you Jimbo?' Conway said, no bitterness in his voice.

'Not employer, partner, fifty – fifty all the way, that right mate?' Warren said.

Jimbo was embarrassed, Mick Conway had done a lot for him, maybe not most of it legal, but he'd looked after him all the same.

'That's right Mick, partners. Thanks for everything but I think it's time for me to move on, know what I mean like? I hope you're ok with that?'

'No problem lad, when you get fed up with working with this twat you just give me the nod. There'll always be a place for you, don't forget it.'

'Thanks Mick, I appreciate that.'

The two men walked the way they had entered, through the back door.

'Well that went better than I expected.' Warren climbed into the Transit and put the case between himself and his young colleague. He flicked open the case and took out two bundles of notes, and stuffed them into his jacket pocket. He thought there were probably around ten thousand pounds, he wasn't really bothered, he already had the extra bonus he'd acquired from Gemmell Strategies, all in all a good wedge he would salt away.

He closed the case and handed it over to Jimbo.

'What do you want me to do with it?'

'It's yours mate.'

'What do you mean it's mine?'

'You said you'd like to get your mum into a decent nursing home, now you can.'

'You can't – I can't accept this!'

'Last time I say this Jimbo, over the past weeks you've saved my neck more than once. If you hadn't watched my back we wouldn't be here now having this argument, so that's it finished. Just put it to good use.'

'Thanks man, I don't know what to say. You don't know just how much difference this money will make. I can't thank you enough,' Jimbo said with teary eyes.

'No thanks needed, you've earned every penny. Now get out the car and piss off.'

'What?'

'Look mate, there's something I've got something to do and there's no need for you to get involved. If things turn out ok I'll be in touch soon, I promise.'

'You said it was a partnership, fifty – fifty…'

'It is, but like I said I've got to do this by myself. Don't worry, I'll be in touch as soon as this is sorted.'

Feeling guilty, he almost had to force Jimbo from the van. He looked in the rear view mirror as he drove away leaving the lad standing on the road edge, holding more money than he'd ever seen in his life.

Warren drove back into the town centre and pulled into the kerb side and turned off the ignition. He sat in the parked van for twenty minutes, debating with himself about what he was going to do, *was he doing the right thing?*

He decided he was.

He got out of the car and left the keys in the ignition – the law of averages said it wouldn't be too long before someone nicked it. The decision was made. He walked around the corner, took a deep breath and walked up the concrete steps, opened the door, walked in and stood in front of the desk.

'Detective Sergeant Greg Warren – Suits and Bullets,' he said to the police officer behind the desk.